Controllers

H.M. Murphy

 Meta IV Pubs

This is a work of fiction. The events and characters portrayed are imaginary. Their resemblance, if any, to real-life counterparts is entirely coincidental.

CONTROLLERS

Published by
Meta IV Pubs
PMB 345
9838 Old Baymeadows Road
Jacksonville, FL 32256

First Printing

All rights reserved
Copyright ©1998 by H.M. Murphy

CONTROLLERS Web Site Address is
http://www.controllersthenovel.com

ISBN: 0-9679538-0-4

Printed in the United States of America
10 9 8 7 6 5 4 3 2 1

Fact: 4,000 FAA senior managers and executives participated in a cult-like training program from 1982 to 1993.

Fact: At least seventy employees from the Office of the Secretary of Transportation attended this training from 1988 to 1993 as did twenty persons from the Office of the Investigator General.

Fact: According to a congressional report, employees of the National Transportation Safety Board were subjected to abusive training in which they were forced to divulge intimate information that would then be used to harass them.

Fact: A two year DOT investigation beginning in March, 1993 found that competitive contracting rules were violated, ethical standards were breached and complaints about the training were ignored by the highest level FAA executives.

Fact: Rep. Frank Wolf, R-Va, said "This was a world where procurement rules were skirted, ethical boundaries were violated, personal and professional lines were blurred beyond recognition, employee privacy was ignored and legitimate concerns of FAA and contract employees were dismissed and even covered up. The training sounded more like fraternity hazing."

Fact: In a televised interview, The DOT Inspector General, Mary Schiavo, said "We were thwarted at many avenues in completing the investigation. A lot of things happened in this which should not happen in a federal agency. There were many activities designed to shut down the investigation, including, at one point trying to have me removed."

This is a work of fiction. The characters and events described here are solely the product of my imagination, and any resemblance to any persons living or dead is purely coincidental. In some cases I make reference to historical events. Where such references are made they are made solely in a fictional context. To those readers who examine fiction for factual anomalies, I have, among other things, largely ignored the organizational structure of the F.A.A. and have taken the artistic liberty of reorganizing it in a manner I thought best suited this story.

Patchwork of America

a story often told, it stands the test of time
of those who've lost their dreams and work the daily grind.
well, I am one of those who stand there in that line
while trying to keep alive the one thing that is mine.

what have I become, where is the dreamer now?
I'd take back that identity if I knew how.
the tears of a man that I all too often wept
as I would recall unspoken promises unkept:

if you're down come to me
I'll take you in and set you free

this modern day caste system's got me locked inside
and I've been stripped of my integrity and pride.
all of my hopeful optimistic views have died
the visionary I used to be was left behind.

if you're down come to me
I'll take you in and set you free
your poor and huddled masses
your broken troubled classes
deliver them to me

I work for the man in the patchwork of america
I've given my whole life to him
I've done all I can in the patchwork of america
herein lies the lie within.[*]

[*] *Lyrics, Patchwork of America, Jon Murphy and Scott Taylor, Tucson, copyright 1996*

*For Bud.
Heroes still exist.*

Acknowledgments

First and foremost, heartfelt gratitude to Bud Murphy for the hours of editing and ideas that were incorporated into the book. To Ann for her strength and support in good times and in bad. To my readers Randy, John, Jeffre, Tricia, Richard and my parents Rose and Lucien. I will be forever grateful for their suggestions and corrections. To Aaron Anderson for his wonderful cover. And finally to my children Jon and Molly. Their passion for life and their creativity helped me through this project.

Chapter One: 1981

"Sooner or later everyone flies. Everyone is vulnerable." Representative Jim Martin faced the flashing lights. The newest member of the FAA oversight committee held his ground as reporters threw questions at him.

"Do you know the cause of yesterday's crash of Flight 172?"

"Is it true that the engine lost a fan blade just before the crash? Sources say that the plane was shaking violently just before it went down."

"Has the death toll been confirmed at 239?"

Martin held up his hands to silence the reporters. "Please. Please." He nodded to a familiar face in the crowd. "As you know, I'm leaving on a fact-finding mission. I will come back with answers to your questions. Count on it." The young Congressman turned and followed the other members of the committee onto the waiting plane.

Moments later Martin settled into a window seat

behind the wing. He was in a somber mood as he reviewed the preliminary report. The facts, at this initial stage, were few. The scene of the crash had been gruesome, the fuselage had sustained catastrophic damage and bodies had been strewn over the crash site. These might, however be caused by the crash itself. One theory, raised by the reporter, was that the engine might have lost a turbine blade. In the industry, this happens more often than the public is made aware of, he mused. A blade, hurtling through the engine can cause fire and engine failure. If it slices through the fuselage it can act like shrapnel. It could also make a large plane shake wildly.

But, there was as yet no data to support this or any theory, he cautioned himself. It would take time to study the chemical residues covering the airplane parts to examine the nature of any fires or explosions. Time to recover and analyze the plane's black box. Until then, they could not rule out anything, including the possibility of terrorism.

Martin's mind continued to explore possibilities. Had an incompetent mechanic overlooked something critical? Had a bogus part been sold to the airline? Was it a matter of the plane being over twenty years old and falling apart? Or had some distracted security guard looked away as a bomb was slipped aboard in the cargo hold? Hell, maybe lightning struck the plane or a bird got sucked into the engine. He frowned and rubbed his forehead as the plane taxied down the runway, preparing for takeoff. The truth was, he didn't know what had caused the failure.

As they accelerated, Martin's eyes were drawn to the wing that had begun to bounce with the unevenness of the runway. Suspended below the wing, just eight feet from him, was a powerful jet engine. He realized with sickening awareness that it was a turbine. The rotations per minute were increasing rapidly. At any moment, a loose blade could turn the engine into a missile capable of slicing through the protective shell around him. He cleared the image from his mind, but his thoughts raced through the plane. All it would take was one bolt not securely tightened. One panel of sheet metal not up to standards. One turbine, not securely fitted.

The roar of engines brought him back to the moment of lift-off and drowned out his thoughts. Martin's grip tightened on the arms of his seat. He prayed.

~

Three weeks later, at the U.S. Army's Ft. Bragg, North Carolina, Captain Jake Morrow waited in the small room as the aide ushered in the ranking officer. General Michael J. Harris had been informed of the case that morning and had insisted on handling it personally. Jake Morrow was one of the bright young lights of the Special Forces. He had been on an assignment of a delicate nature that had kept him out of the country for the past few months. Having arrived stateside a few short hours ago, Jake had been thoroughly debriefed about his mission. He wondered what the delay was that prevented him from leaving for home. Harris studied the young man's handsome face. He cleared his throat.

"It's an honor to meet you, young man." After returning the captain's salute, the general reached out and shook the young man's hand. "Please, have a seat."

Jake nodded acknowledgment, but remained standing.

"I have some bad news for you, son. Three weeks ago, Pan World Airlines, Flight 172 crashed. All passengers on board were killed. Son, your wife and baby were on that flight. I'm so sorry."

The General stood by quietly as the life slowly drained from Jake's eyes.

The heat in the Pittsburgh foundry was sweltering. The summer sun beating on the roof compounded the misery of those inside.

"A turbine engine is an example of a controlled explosion," the operations manager was explaining, wiping his face with a handkerchief. "The jet-driven turbine consists of four basic parts: compressor, combustion chambers, turbine and propelling nozzles. In the combustion chambers the combustion of a fuel, mixed with air coming from the compressor, generates expanding gases, which spin the rotor of the turbine. The axis of the turbine is connected by a shaft directly to the axis of the compressor; thus the turbine drives the compressor. The gas, after passing through the turbine, is exhausted into the atmosphere through a nozzle at high speed. It's all about thrust." He smiled at his own cleverness.

A hand went up in the sweaty but dedicated group made up mostly of Representative Martin's entourage.

"Yes? The Asian student." The operations manager nodded.

Bill Lee's irritation was expressed by a single, almost imperceptible, blink. He had been born and raised in the United States and he resented being labeled. In fact, his father, an American, was distantly related to Robert E. Lee. But, because he favored his Japanese-born mother, people presumed it must be Bruce Lee. Bill cleared his throat. He took his summer job as a page for Representative Martin very seriously.

"What's the weakest point in the engine?" He asked.

The operations manager squinted to see the young challenger, pencil and pad in hand. "There are several possible trouble spots," he responded. "One is the point at which the blades attach to the engine. Another is the composition of the blades themselves.

"They are made from the finest grade titanium. Each blade is drop forged. That is the process of taking slightly cooled metal, almost like putty, and stamping it into the right shape. The metal then goes through an annealing process."

He saw the young man's hand and anticipated the question. "Annealing is what you do to make metal tough. The key to the process is how you cool the metal down. The difference between hard and tough is critical in terms of safety standards. If you cool titanium too quickly it gets hard. Cool it slowly and it gets tough."

"So a hard titanium blade is brittle," Bill Lee said.

"Yes. That's why the annealing process is so

critical. It takes longer and costs more, but the end result is a tough, durable blade able to sustain great pressure."

"Is it possible to forge low grade titanium blades?"

"It's possible to cast the liquid metal instead of forging it and skip the annealing process altogether. The result is a lot cheaper, and much less safe."

"How can you tell the difference between the two?" Lee pressed.

The operations manager looked at him. "You ask tough questions, son."

Chapter Two: Beginnings

An August morning that promised to break 110° in the shade persuaded Jake Morrow to mount his Harley and head for Mt. Lemmon. He left Tucson and the suffocating monsoon air quickly behind. As he ascended, winding back and forth up the side of the mountain, he noticed the vegetation begin to change as prickly pear gave way to brush, then the first hint of cooler, pine-scented air blew past his collar length hair. He hadn't been to a barber since the accident three months earlier. He'd bought a bike after leaving the force and had been wandering around the country trying to figure out what to do with the rest of his life.

Two young women in a red convertible waved playfully as Jake passed them on the narrow road that had been painstakingly carved out of the area's highest mountain. There was something in the set of his chiseled jaw and the cool intensity of his eyes that intimidated men and caused women to take a second look. He had the appearance of a man completely focused on the present, because there was little comfort for him in the past or hope in the future. Halfway up the mountain, Jake stopped at a scenic lookout. He steadied the bike with his left foot and shaded his eyes with his hands, studying the city below.

He liked Tucson as well as any place he'd seen. It was an odd mix of cowboys and culture, of beauty and ugliness. Local Indian legends added an air of mystery and romance to the valley that was surrounded on all sides by mountain ranges. Each evening the setting sun would burnish everything in its path, creating a sense of living energy in every rock, in every creature. In this world, the tall saguaros dotting the valleys and foothills were vigilant sentries with ancient souls. It was a haven for the lost — and the seekers.

Jake had spent the day before taking a tour of the "graveyard" which covered countless acres, all filled with mothballed planes of varied vintage. If they were all activated, they would form the third largest air force on earth. The dry desert air and hard soil made it an ideal location to store and preserve planes. Jake had enjoyed the day, in spite of the oppressive heat. Planes had never been one of his passions, but now they pulled at him. From his mountain view, he looked for the plane graveyard, but it was behind foothills to the Southeast. He could see most of the valley stretched out below, surrounded by the Catalinas to the North, the Tucson Mountains to the West and the Santa Ritas and Chiricahuas to the South. The Rincons reaching up behind him closed the circle.

Noticing the rumblings in his stomach, Jake cranked his bike to life and continued upward, absorbed in the pleasure of leaning deep into the turns. As he passed the first scattering of cabins near Summerhaven, he spotted a small diner that looked inviting. There were several vehicles in the parking lot, among them a red pickup truck. A pretty, young mother with long black hair, little more than a girl herself, was nestled in the back of the truck next to a large picnic basket. She cradled twin little dark-eyed girls in each arm. The babies were dressed exactly alike, except that in their pierced ears one wore the tiniest red earrings, and the other wore green. They babbled cheerfully, content to be waiting for their driver, having escaped the heat of the desert floor.

Jake parked the bike out front, went in and sat at the counter. Two young Native-Americans were standing by the cash register with a case of soda pop. They were smiling and engaged in friendly banter as they waited for the waitress to ring up their bill. One of them must be the driver of the truck, he thought.

Suddenly, from the parking lot came the squeal of tires. The young men turned, then bolted out the door yelling. "Stop! Come back!" Someone was stealing their truck with its innocent occupants and was heading back down the mountain.

Jake was out the door and on his bike without thinking. As he closed on the truck, he hung back, not wanting to threaten it's reckless hijackers — from the wild way they were driving they had to be high on something. They probably didn't even realize they had passengers on board. The truck bobbed and weaved. It was now about 10:00 in the morning and there was a steady stream of cars and recreational vehicles coming up from the desert below. A tired looking, dust-covered station wagon filled with Cub Scouts had stalled, and a deputy sheriff was directing traffic around them. When he saw the speeding truck fly by and heard the woman's screams for help he jumped into his car, turned on his sirens and screeched after them.

Jake noticed a crushed picnic basket, its contents scattered along the side of the road. The sheriff's car approached from behind and Jake pulled aside letting it pass. The truck picked up speed. Turns were becoming harder for it to navigate as it barreled forward. Suddenly its way was blocked by a large van attempting to pass slower cars coming up the mountain. The driver of the truck slammed on the brakes and swerved to avoid hitting the van, sending the truck sliding off the road.

Jake saw it stop, its front end suspended over the side of the mountain, its back tires still on solid ground. The left front tire was wedged between two large rocks, the right was spinning in the air. The babies were screaming, held in one arm by their mother, who was hanging onto the side of the rocking truck with all her strength.

The deputy screeched his patrol car to a stop and was attempting to get his shotgun freed from its bracket on the dash. As Jake pulled up he figured the truck had less than a minute before its weight pulled it free and sent it toppling to the valley floor below. He winced as he leapt from his bike and let it fall on its side, not wasting time to set it down. Running to the truck, he leaned forward, and in a controlled voice said to the mother,

"Hand me one of the babies." Her eyes were moist with terror, but realizing the extent of the danger, she grabbed one girl by the back of her little dress and pushed her forward. She held onto the side with the other arm and her other baby with her legs.

Jake grabbed the girl and, quickly looking behind him, tossed her into the arms of the deputy, who had abandoned his shotgun and had arrived to help. Jake leaned back toward the truck.

"Good, now the other." Just then the truck groaned and swayed. But it held. The woman was trembling, looking down at the side of the mountain yawning beneath the truck. Jake looked at her calmly.

"Look at me!" His voice was firm. She turned to him and nodded. "All right — now!" She handed him the remaining child. He passed the other child to another bystander who had run up to help. By now the bloodied and sobered thieves realized their situation and had begun to panic, their movements making the truck sway precariously.

"Don't move!" Jake cried to them, but they were beyond listening. He focused on the girl.

"Grab my hand." She reached out, but at that moment the truck swayed away and she could not reach him. He had to get closer. Slipping off his jacket and using it like a rope, he tossed one sleeve to the deputy, who caught it and held on with both hands. The deputy leaned back, digging his heels into the ground and used his weight as a counterbalance. Using the added leverage, Jake reached out once more.

"Let's try again. Hold on." She reached for him and he grabbed her arm just before the truck's tire groaned out of its rocky vice and disappeared over the side of the mountain. Her body was dead weight as she hung helplessly over the edge. Jake held his ground as the girl's weight strained every muscle. Slowly he pulled her up until she lay safely on the ground. He stepped back as her husband rushed to her side.

Later that day Jake stopped by the emergency room lobby to find out how everyone was doing. The father, a young man called Joseph, and his kid brother Louis wouldn't stop thanking him. They jabbered on, sometimes in English, sometimes in a language unfamiliar to Jake, retelling the story to each new relative who entered the waiting room. Soon the girls were brought out. They had come through the entire ordeal with scarcely a mark. Finally, a nurse wheeled the young mother into the lobby. Her right arm and shoulder were bound up in bandages, and packed with ice. The doctor came out and explained that it probably had been dislocated, and that she had a bad sprain.

Mary, as he now knew her, was talking quietly to her father, a tall, imposing man who had just arrived. She asked him to wheel her over to Jake. Her father grasped Jake's hand with gratitude. Somewhat shyly, Mary looked up at this stranger who had risked his life for her and her children.

"I know we can never thank you enough for what you did." She smiled. "But please, keep this always as a way to remember what you mean to us." She handed him a neatly folded tissue.

Later that night, in his hotel room, under a solitary light, Jake took the gift from his pocket and unfolded it. There, laying in the folds of the tissue, were two tiny earrings, one red and one green. His eyes moistened as he stared at them.

~

There was no place on earth the man felt more alive and more whole. This was his sanctuary. He returned year after year to drink deep of the redwoods -- of their smell, their unique sounds and silences. He had first been invited to the lodge shortly after college graduation. Over the years as the pressures and complexities of his public and political life increased, he sought this refuge with a quiet desperation. He needed the distance from Washington, from the prying eyes of his enemies. He longed for the closeness of old friends. Of equals.

That afternoon he had gone for a long walk around the outer perimeter of the complex, secured by barbed wire fencing that disappeared into the foliage. He passed sentries, some with guard dogs, at regular intervals. These men stood like shadows, eyes averted, giving him his space, knowing their place.

Now he looked forward to his favorite part of the day. It was cool in the evening at this elevation in Northern California, even in summer. As he went downstairs to the main hall of the lodge he knew he would be greeted by a crackling fire and the conversation of old friends. His eyes gazed around the walls and he nodded almost unconsciously. He viewed them with respect, these regal heads mounted with care. Each one was a testament to the skill of its hunter. Not a one had been taken by bullet -- all bow and arrow kills. A fair hunt. An even playing field. Their eyes open, they seemed frozen forever in that final moment of consciousness, as though destined for perpetual awareness. They were proper symbols of the battle for survival, and proof that in any conflict — there always is a loser. He felt strangely comfortable, almost protected by them, as they watched, year after year.

He was welcomed by the scent of exquisite cigars and smooth Scotch. These were the few indulgences that they allowed each other. Tonight was a special treat for him. He had something on his mind and had come a day early. He needed to talk with a few close confidants. He shook his head wryly as he realized that even here, among friends, there were only a few that he could really trust.

He saw two of them already comfortably settled on the massive couch that faced the fireplace. He went over to an enormous winged armchair that faced them, but which still allowed him to keep an eye on the door.

"Admiral," he said warmly, leaning forward, extending his arm and grasping his old friend's hand. The old man smiled back, revealing a set of bad teeth that his wife and daughter had for years urged him to get capped. There was no way. Of all things, the admiral, decorated countless times for bravery in action and scarred from a lifetime of conflict, was terrified of dentists. He had admitted this to his friend once in an unusually open moment. Now, every time the admiral smiled, his friend smiled too.

The occupant of the winged chair turned slightly.

"And you, Richard," he greeted him warmly. "How goes the Trust?" Sir Richard Burroughs, man of letters, patron of the arts and knighted by the queen was passionately committed to the oversight of the Castaneda Trust he had founded in 1971. Its lofty purpose was to promote spiritual knowledge and education. He was highly regarded by fellow New Age thinkers for his experiments in community living, for promoting interest in pilgrimages to ancient sacred places, and for sponsoring a variety of research projects.

The trust was heavily endowed. Benefactors included varied sources, individual bequests, as well as MI-5 funded special research programs. The latter's support was kept well hidden, however, and the man facing Sir Richard chuckled at the delicious deception of using such an operation for some of his own favorite projects.

He had benefited from the trust during the late 70's when he had been privately tutored in neurolinguistics. He had been impressed. It was amazing what you could read from a person's eye patterns -- could tell when they were lying, what they were feeling, when they were resisting. The whole pacing and leading thing had turned out to be quite valuable to him as a public figure -- get on the group's wave length and then take charge of the trip. That had been the beginning. Then he had studied Ericksonian hypnosis, developed by the followers of Milton Erickson who could hypnotize a group by his simple act of walking across a stage. He was much loved by his students who tried to imitate and systematize his unique style. Amazing how easy it was to lead a group, Skippy mused. One had to be subtle, though. Being obvious could be dangerous when the stakes were so high.

He felt grateful to Richard. The man had personally been in charge of arranging for his training, and had been most discrete.

Richard smiled back. "The trust is doing smashingly, Skippy, as you predicted."

Skippy nodded acknowledgment. These were the only men he allowed to call him by the nickname, derived from his almost embarrassingly short stint as a naval skipper in the war. He leaned forward, poured himself some Scotch and then sipped it slowly, leaning back against the soft chair, letting the heat of it spread slowly over his tongue and down the back of his throat. He became aware of the crackling of the wood in the fireplace.

At that moment the massive front door of the lodge opened, and in walked the final member of the invited group.

"Well, well, Henry. Come in, man. How was your flight?"

"Fine, thank you, gentlemen." Henry, the billionaire telecommunications giant, smiled. Giant was an incongruous description. The man was not 5'5" and possessed the small, wiry constitution bequeathed him by generations of energetic, hard working entrepreneurs. His eyes were bright and his blinks, timed with his head movements gave others the distinct impression of a bird, for those who knew him well, a bird of prey. Henry proceeded to perch on the arm of the remaining seat, an upholstered easy chair.

Skippy leaned forward and began. "Gentlemen, let's get right to it. The situation is now critical. You all know that Bonzo's fired the striking controllers. It's been a nightmare." He frowned and leaned forward, looking at the admiral. "Had to go along with it. Never want to go through this again. Such a total waste."

The admiral nodded gravely. "Morale, sir," he stated, dropping the diminutive, Skippy, to reflect the seriousness of the matter, "is very low. But the controller's union was asking for it. They had gotten too goddamn big for their britches."

"Don't blame it all on the union. Men are by nature followers, and if the FAA had leaders instead of managers with one eye on retirement and the other on the golf course, it would never have come to this. How can we assume that men who have come up the ranks separating planes or inspecting radar equipment will know how to lead?"

Richard cleared his throat. "You know, this might be the opportunity we've been waiting for." There was a silence. "The FAA would be a perfect laboratory to test our research. Since our first soldiers were captured in Korea, we've been studying brainwashing techniques to find ways to combat it. Ways to deprogram our boys when they came home. Along the way we've developed a significant body of work on the techniques of mind control. A most interesting by-product of our efforts." He looked at them, waiting for the thought to take hold. "Theory isn't worth the paper it's written on, gentlemen. It needs to be tested."

The admiral frowned, "Are you saying we should brainwash our own men, Richard? Do I have to remind you we live in a democracy? It wouldn't be tolerated."

"No, not brainwash." Skippy jumped in. "This is about providing real leadership. Don't you see? You've got to admit that democracy is the most inefficient form of government. Without true leadership, our democracy will crumble. It's as simple as that. Just look around, our country's a mess, just like the agency. I'm convinced that controllers, like most citizens want to do good, they just don't know what that is. They look to their leaders to tell them."

"But you've just said they have no effective

leadership." The admiral was clearly uncomfortable.

"Yes I did. That's why it's up to us to provide them with leaders. Leaders with true values, like integrity and accountability. Leaders that they can look up to, admire and emulate. We need to create a team of leaders, first in the FAA — then in the rest of government. Actually, the reason I've invited Henry here today is to bring us all up to speed on his experiments with leadership training — one advantage the private sector has over us government types. Henry, what have you learned so far from Project Empowerment?"

Henry shot to his feet. "Actually, quite a bit. I can summarize it in three points. First, since we are essentially talking about how men cope with change, the key was to break down their resistance to change in their own lives. This can be a challenge. Some personalities are more rigid than others, and it takes a concerted effort for those individuals to break through to a new way of seeing themselves and the world, to a new paradigm. Their personalities must be rebuilt with care, and it appears to work best in a group environment. We've had great success using peer pressure to reinforce the kinds of behavioral changes we're after. In fact, there appears to be an almost exponential impact when we use group pressure. It's particularly effective to plant our specially trained people in the group, posing as ordinary members. The group appears to have less defense against one of their own.

"Secondly, we now have a clear profile of the type of personality most likely to resist our techniques. This insight is of great value. It allows us to cut to the chase and eliminate those folks quickly, before they have a negative influence on the group."

Skippy interrupted. "What's the profile?"

"Originally we had pinpointed people with military backgrounds and fundamentalists with an exaggerated sense of right and wrong. They do form one large, somewhat resistant group, but we've learned to work with them effectively. While they have strong loyalties to something other than themselves, we've found that these loyalties can be swayed. The profile that is most troublesome to us is the loner. The rebel. This person has underdeveloped corporate thinking. Relies too much on his own perceptions. It's better to cut and cut fast with this type.

"Which brings me to the third and most important point." Henry paused for a moment, letting their curiosity build. "The third thing we have learned, is that we can't afford to start with the people at the bottom. They might appeal to their supervisors or unions for support. No — this thing has got to be done top down. As the project grows and trickles downward, there'll be nowhere to appeal. No move to make, but to comply or get out, and the few that get out will have nowhere to turn."

Skippy nodded. "What we need is someone who can handle it. Someone who can invisibly and completely take control of the project."

~

It was a simply furnished office, one of many professional suites in the heart of the Beltway. The usual desk, a few chairs facing each other, a comfortable sofa and several bookshelves. Along the walls were numerous degrees and awards reflecting the impressive pedigree of Dr. Elizabeth Caldwell.

Throughout her years of research, Dr. Caldwell had maintained a private practice, honing her skills, testing her theories. Her life was consumed by her work, except for rare breaks every few years during which she would get married or have a brief but torrid affair. She seemed either unable or unwilling to integrate her two worlds. Currently separated from her fourth husband, she was deeply involved in her latest project.

Caldwell had through the years developed a deep conviction that people were lost children at heart, cut off from their full potential and adrift in a sea of distortion and fear. Further, she had come to believe that it was not their fault. Society had let them down. Parents were too busy earning money to provide guidance for their kids; schools were hampered by regulations; institutions, paralyzed by red tape. She viewed people as essentially orphans in need of adequate parenting — and they weren't getting it from society.

Her specialty was the treatment of character disorders. Unlike the more common neurotic these individuals' defenses became part of their personality. The defense was the personality. She was intrigued by the challenge of dealing with this type of individual, because it required of her the toughness of a drill sergeant, the authority of a four star general and the ability to create feelings of shame, a skill that appears innate in some women.

If there was anyone who possessed the requisite variety needed for this task, it was Elizabeth Caldwell, a master hypnotist thoroughly schooled in the basic as well as esoteric techniques of mind control, tools much needed when dealing with difficult populations. She had learned much from her research: the use of sensory and sleep deprivation, altered diet, the withdrawal of caffeine and sugars. Those were the basics. Further, she was a master of the yes set, skilled at posing questions and creating situations which demanded the desired response from the client, a kind of slippery slope of adaptation. It was the most basic of hypnotic inductions and set a context for "learning". She had learned to play groups like a conductor plays an orchestra — pulling for heightened effort and outpouring from some, while skillfully silencing others. It was an art, and she was gifted.

But today was different. Andrew had been in her care for years. Seven years ago he had been given a choice of therapy or reform school by a juvenile court judge, and had chosen shrewdly. Andrew Maxwell, the spoiled son of wealthy parents, had in some way been implicated in their apparent accidental deaths. His family's wealth and influence had kept him out of the public eye, and thanks to therapy, he had grown up without any lasting shadows over his reputation.

Caldwell knew better, however. It had taken her years to break through, and what she had found wasn't pretty. But she worked hard and her efforts finally produced an outwardly compliant adult. She was proud of her work. The child had become a man.

Andrew was now in his mid twenties and had sun-bleached curly hair and relentlessly observant eyes. He had gone on to college and completed one Ph.D. in psychology and was picking up another in physics in his spare time.

Dr. Caldwell listened quietly to him now. Her eyes, like water, mirrored his changing emotions. The delicacy of her nose and chin formed a deceptively fragile profile that she would, on occasion use to her advantage, while her shoulder length blond hair, clear skin and hazel eyes created a neutral palette that allowed clients to form whatever image they needed as they faced their own private demons.

On this day Andrew had come to tell her that the FAA had offered him a position in their training department. As he spoke of his ambitions and plans, she listened intently, having long ago learned to leave theory and logic behind during a session. She, and she alone was the tool she wielded in the present moment. As Andrew got ready to leave, her eyes conveyed her pride and something more nebulous. He had become a striking man, well positioned to do whatever he chose. She played with a strand of her hair that lay along her shoulder.

As he reached the door, he turned back, looked at her and stopped, his eyes boring into hers. He had lusted after her for years, but today the signs were unmistakable. In one large step he reached her, grabbed her hair and pulled back her head. He kissed her throat and then her mouth. She pulled back, pushing him away with her arms and struck him across the cheek, her eyes blazing, her lips parted. Andrew looked at her a moment and laughed. Locking the door behind him, he turned and walked deliberately toward her. He picked her up and carried her to the couch.

~

Danielle O'Malley stood at the sink of her tiny apartment and finished the last few dishes. Hanging the washcloth on the cupboard door to dry, she carried two sets of dishes over to the small, metal table, flanked by two metal chairs. She smiled as she carefully set the table, her eyes revealing a hint of Irish triumph toying with her native Italian skepticism. She put a pot of water on to boil and congratulated herself on making it through the entire week on her own. Last Friday, at exactly 10 a.m. she had walked out of her convent life for good.

The decision had been a difficult one. Orphaned after her parents' deaths when she was only five, Dani had been passed around various foster homes until she entered the convent at seventeen. The nuns had given her a feeling of belonging and purpose, and she had gradually acquired a discipline and focus that few would have thought possible, given her lonely and somewhat rebellious teenage years. She had completed high school and then college and had recently won a scholarship for graduate school, when she finally faced the fact that she wasn't meant for convent life. There had to be something more to life and she meant to find out what.

Under the circumstances, the nuns had been kind. They had pressed $250.00 into her hands and offered up prayers for her soul. She had saved up the checks her foster parents had sent during the past year, and the first thing she did was open a bank account. Her walk to the bank had been an eye opener. She felt unexpectedly invisible. While in her habit, she had walked down streets greeted by warm smiles. People would meet her eyes, nod and every so often someone would grab her hand and ask for a prayer, as though the contact alone would count in some heavenly ledger. Even the rare person who seemed frightened by nuns at least acknowledged her existence. Now, in ordinary clothes, with her new crop of short brown hair, she seemed invisible. The world had abruptly become a more complicated place.

Her second task had been to find a little efficiency near campus, so she could continue graduate work at Georgetown. It had taken her only a few hours, newspaper in hand, to secure the apartment. Poor was the word that best fit her new environment, but it was her poverty now, and she had smiled contentedly as she stepped inside and leaned momentarily on the security of the closed door behind her. Beside the kitchen table and two chairs was a Murphy bed that folded down from the wall. The stains and rips in the mattress revealed years of tenant abuse. When she could, she would replace it. Along the other wall was a worn, brown plaid sofa. It was plain to the point of being ugly, but it was comfortable.

As she poured herself tea and sat somewhat formally on the sofa, her eyes explored the room. All around the wall, in every available space, lay bookshelves made of plain pine boards and cinder blocks, standard issue for students everywhere. This was already a new ritual for her. Every evening for a week she sat, drinking tea and looking around the apartment. Anticipation was one of her favorite feelings and she hadn't yet tired of the activity. She found herself replaying the small surge of excitement that occurred when she pictured her life that was just beginning, without the habit to protect her. The new semester would be starting in a few days, and she had a lot to do to get ready. Suddenly, the doorbell rang. She felt uneasy, wondering who it could be.

"Do you have any sugar?" A loud voice from the hallway called out. She opened the door to see her neighbor, a young oriental student she had noticed the other day. He moved right past her into the apartment.

"Hi! Bill Lee. Journalism. Remember? I met you in the hall yesterday. What's your name again?"

"Oh, Hi, Bill. Nice to meet you — my name is — Dani." She had paused to remind herself that she no longer was Sister Marie de Lourdes. "I do have some sugar. How much do you need?"

Bill handed her a small cup to fill. He noticed the table set for two. "Sorry if I'm interrupting," he said nodding toward the table.

"No, that's all right. I'm not expecting anyone."

"That's strange," Bill replied brusquely. "If you're not expecting anyone, why is the table set for two?" He looked straight at her.

Dani wasn't used to such directness. It caught her off guard. "I guess it's a habit. I've just left the convent," she stammered. "And, well — we used to set the table after dishes for the next meal. It's actually rather efficient," she added defensively.

"It's not efficient, it's pathetic." His beautiful

almond eyes conveyed amazement. "You mean to tell me you always set the table ahead? What if you go out to eat? And why is it set for two? Don't you live here alone?"

"Well, yes I do, so what? What business is it of yours, anyway?" Dani retorted, her Irish temper slipping out.

Bill looked at her and then back at the table. "How can you be spontaneous at all? I mean, what if you wanted to play chess? You'd have to put it all away." He took the sugar from her hands, mumbled thanks, and left just as fast as he had come.

After she locked the door, she walked toward the kitchen and stared at the table, hands folded as in prayer, both index fingers pressed against her lips. She wanted to think this through. Partly, she supposed, she had been comforted by the familiar ritual. She felt a slight flush of embarrassment, that not too frequent feeling that occurred when she realized something about herself that she might not like to know. Okay, she admitted to herself, maybe she hadn't wanted to face the fact that she was all alone in the world again. It was understandable that she might be reluctant to come to grips with that. She put the dishes and silverware back into the cupboards. Gazing uncomfortably at the now empty table, she wondered what she would do for breakfast.

Later that night in the dark, safely tucked into the old Murphy bed, Dani O'Malley replayed the events of the day and smiled. So it begins, she thought.

Chapter Three: Ten Years Later

Dani paused to let her eyes adjust to the darkness as she entered the Los Angeles Terminal Radar Approach Control Facility, or LAX TRACON for short. Sid Jones, the manager on duty, stepped aside and watched her as she moved into the strange, dimly lit world filled with rows of radar consoles and a muffled buzz of activity. He never tired of the look of fascination that inevitably spread over visitor's faces. This woman with her thick hair in a French braid, smooth skin and trim figure was a pleasure to look at regardless of the situation.

In front of each scope men and women wearing headsets were intently occupied with the business of keeping planes separated and providing a safe, orderly and expeditious flow of air traffic, or in the vernacular, 'pushing tin'. Some were standing, others sitting and shifting quickly back and forth on chairs, coordinating information with each other. Sid led her down a row of consoles, introducing her to various controllers and explaining what area of air space each was responsible for. He went on ahead, then called her forward.

"Dani," he said, with his hand on the shoulder of a man in his late twenties, casually but neatly dressed like most controllers in short sleeved shirts and slacks. "I'd like you to meet Tom Nowicki. He's one of the people you'll be shadowing, excuse me, working with for the next few days."

Tom grinned and held out his hand, "Glad to meet you, Dani. And this," he said, nodding in the direction of an attractive African-American woman, "is Etta Young. She's a developmental and you'll get a chance to observe some OJT."

Etta nodded but kept her eyes on the display in front of her. She spoke clearly into the microphone, "Delta 2493, descend and maintain 2,000."

Sid explained. "OJT is on the job training — as you probably know the FAA is heavy into acronyms. We'll drive you crazy with acronyms." He laughed. "But I think you'll see how necessary they are here. Controllers and pilots use standard phraseology. They have to use language that everyone in the business understands. Lives are riding on being understood clearly and concisely."

"Sid, do you think it's wise for me to be assigned to Tom? Won't it be distracting for him to have to worry about me when he's training?" Dani asked.

"I understand your concern," Sid replied. "But one thing you'll soon observe about controllers is that they can follow several conversations at once. I've been told it's disturbing at first to try to converse with us. We'll be talking to you, handle a couple transactions with pilots, finish the sentence where we left off and squeeze in a bit of banter with the guy at the next position. Hopefully, you'll get used to it." He chuckled.

"The technology you have in this room is really impressive." Dani's eyes focused on the screens around the room.

"Well — it works. Though our air traffic control system is the safest in the world, much of the hardware, like the Automated Radar Terminal System III - we call it the ARTS3 - that we use to track targets and display data to the controllers is hopelessly behind the technological curve. Come with me. I want to show you what I mean." Sid led Dani out of the main room. They followed a long narrow hallway into another section of the hangar that had been put into service to house the TRACON when ARTS3 was first installed. Sid stopped in front of two large grey doors.

"I'd like to introduce you to the guts of our air control system." Sid ushered her into a room stacked with rows of computers, wires, tubes and flashing lights. "Most of the technology in here is over 25 years old. It was installed in the late sixties and here it sits. Look at these antiques." He shook his head and looked around the room. "We've been trying to upgrade this equipment for decades, but it's such a complex task that by the time any upgrade is coordinated it's already out of date. Actually, I think Washington would love to replace all the controllers with some advanced system, but they just haven't figured how to get from here to there yet."

"I've heard that the system keeps crashing. Isn't that dangerous?" Dani asked.

"You bet it is. It's a miracle more people haven't been killed. O'Hare and Miami experience regular power failures. Actually, outages all across the country are much more common than the FAA lets on. When the system fails, its traumatic, to say the least. And depending what the failure is; radar, ARTS3, commercial power; whatever, the controllers regroup around the best fall-back mode for the particular failure and keep 'em separated and movin'."

"Exactly what happens when the ARTS3 fails?"

"Actually, the screens lose only the alphanumeric

data. The facility reverts to basic radar control which is traumatic enough because the controller suddenly loses all real-time references to speeds, altitudes and other important data. As a result, it's chaos until basic radar procedures are established and the brain shifts gears."

Dani nodded, following Sid's explanation. "What if there's a power failure?"

Sid raised his eyebrows. "When commercial power fails, the scopes blank out - unless an uninterruptable power supply (UPS) has been installed. If the radios and telephones still work, the facility tries to revert to manual (non-radar) control with the help of nearby facilities and the associated ARTCC. Most of the big-time high profile outages have been power failures."

"I guess you never know, do you?"

Sid paused a moment. "No you never do. I guess that's why we have to maintain a constant manual backup system. We can never really predict when one controller's ability to think for himself will be the difference between disaster and survival."

~

Harry Peterson's name plaque was the only thing that distinguished his desk from all the others on the 7th floor of the FAA's building in the heart of the nation's capital. Managers were a dime a dozen in this top-heavy headquarters. His office consisted of a chair, a desk and stacks of books, papers, file folders and whatever, piled in such a way as to create a sense of place amid the rubble that was the contracts office. Harry had a long and somewhat undistinguished career and was looking forward to retirement in six months.

He was still at his desk even though it was now 4:30 p.m. and most of the Washington work force was on its way to the Metro or carpools for the tedious trek home. Harry scratched his head and brushed the doughnut crumbs from the ledge of his overgenerous stomach. He hesitated, then finished all but the dregs of a cold cup of coffee from the vending machine in the hall. He went over the figures again, a worried frown creasing his balding forehead. He spread several sheets out over the mess on his desk so he could compare numbers. It was undeniable. A pattern was emerging from the senior executive training program that he thought needed to be brought to someone's attention.

This made him uncomfortable. He was not one to

challenge the status quo. He was too near retirement and just plain tired. Maybe he should overlook this pattern of contracting irregularities, he had thought at first. But in the 2:00 p.m. mail he had received an anonymous manila envelope. This disturbed Harry, because in his experience, on the few occasions that anything out of the ordinary occurred it usually led to trouble. He had slipped the envelope into his bottom drawer and locked it without really knowing why. At the end of the day, as the office started to clear out, he knew he had to open it in spite of his foreboding.

After looking around to be sure he was alone, he took it out of the locked drawer. Reaching into the envelope he removed the contents. Two articles from the Post lay on his desk. One was a short, slightly yellowed news column, the other, an obituary.

Where'd this come from, he wondered. And why would anyone send it to me?

The article was about a training program that had taken place six years ago at the IRS. Allegedly as a result of participating in management training run by a Dr. Elizabeth Caldwell, two participants had committed suicide. No conclusions were drawn by the writer of the article. The training program had been quietly canceled.

But Harry's heart pounded when he saw the

obituary. There was a picture of Tom Brown, a buddy he used to work with from Oklahoma, also approaching the 25 year mark. How had it happened? He remembered Tom calling him almost a year ago.

"They think I'm a dinosaur, Harry." He had laughed, but his voice sounded distressed. "They're sending me to exec school to get my spine removed. You'd better watch out," he warned. "You'll be next. They're out to get rid of all of us dinosaurs. At this rate we'll be extinct pretty soon. At least I'll get a break from work for two weeks."

That was the last time he had talked to Tom. He heard later, from a colleague who had attended the same session, that Tom had acted like a jerk. He had been unwilling to participate. He just didn't get it, claimed the colleague. Henry had wondered at the time what it was, but then he forgot about the entire incident. Later that month Tom had retired, 6 months early and no retirement party. It seemed strange to Harry, but he had been too busy to call and find out more. So there it was. What the hell did it all mean?

~

Like clockwork, the thunderheads had begun to boil in the afternoon heat and were stalking across the valley from the south. It was 4:00 in the afternoon. By 4:30 the Tucson valley would be assaulted by torrential rains and violent lightning, an almost daily summer monsoon ritual. The three men in the tower cab braced themselves. Things would be popping for them any minute.

Jim, the youngest, a recent college grad in navy slacks and a well worn Arizona Wildcat's T-shirt was working local control, doing what he could to keep the novice pilots of the airport's flight school from pranging into each other, the ground or the four mountain ranges circling the valley like lazy giants sprawled out on the desert floor. Jim was standing, turning constantly to maintain visual and radio contact with the students, who were trying to fit in one last touch and go before the storm arrived. Jim loved every minute of the game that was ATC.

Fred, an old-timer with an amazingly large, pockmarked red nose, was working the data position, doing the routine housework that keeps a shift up-to-date with the rest of the world. This included monitoring the Albuquerque Air Route Traffic Control Center; Tucson's own radar control facility, housed at nearby Davis Monthan Air Force Base; the Weather Service; the Flight Service Station and all the 'ships at sea'.

Jake was the third, the tower supervisor on duty. His brown hair was pulled back at the neck and he wore neatly pressed khaki slacks, cowboy boots and a cream-colored shirt with the sleeves rolled-up. A closer look revealed two small earrings in his left ear. He stood at the back of the cab discussing the recent performance of the tower's BRITE radar display with Herman Tallhorse, one of the maintenance sector's radar techs.

Herman could talk with Jake about technical matters, something he couldn't say about the other ATC supervisors. They were content to complain about equipment problems, rather than give the in-depth analysis he could expect from Jake. The glare from the scorching, bright desert sun created the worst of all environments to get easily discernible targets from the BRITE, much like watching TV in the backyard on a sunny day. Even though they both knew it was operating to specifications, Jake realized that talking the situation through with Herman would result in improved performance. Unknown to either of them, a situation was beginning to develop.

Early that morning, in the dark, Duke Winters had

carefully scanned the instrument panel of his prized old Taylorcraft. Everything was as it should be. He loved the old plane that he had discovered at an airshow in Florida, and he had spent years getting it into top shape. He had complete confidence in the reliability of the machine. His eyes gleamed with pride as he turned to the young man. "She's all yours, son."

"Thanks, Dad." Dave Winters, a junior at Embry-Riddle Aeronautical University in Daytona Beach was about to undertake his first solo, long-distance flight. He was heading out to Tucson to celebrate his sister's 18th birthday. His father would take a commercial flight out of Daytona Beach for a morning meeting scheduled in Tucson. Then, later in the day, his dad would meet him at the Tucson Airport.

During the flight, Dave had time to review his preparations. The Taylorcraft was generally regarded as an antique with an interesting history. Through the years, various companies had purchased the plans and production rights, and there seemed to be two different iterations of the plane. One version was regarded as an alternative to the Piper Cub. It had 65 horsepower, held 12 gallons of usable fuel and could travel at 95 m.p.h.. Its range was limited to 182 miles. His Dad's plane, however, fit into a different category. It had 118 horsepower. It held 40 gallons of fuel and could reach speeds of 122 m.p.h.. It also had a much broader range and could travel up to 722 miles without refueling.

It was about 1,600 miles from Daytona Beach up to Jacksonville, then over to Pensacola and on to Tucson. Dave had planned his stops very carefully, avoiding long distances over the Gulf or unpopulated swamp areas. He was beginning to understand why most antique aircraft owners make few long distance trips. He had calculated that he would need at least three refueling stops. Given that each stop could take an hour or more, if he maintained maximum cruising speed, the trip should take just over 13 hours. Further, it was summer, and Arizona did not change to daylight savings time along with the rest of the country. That meant they were two hours earlier than Daytona. So, if his goal was to arrive in Tucson by 4 in the afternoon and avoid running into the predictable monsoon storms, he needed to take off from Daytona by 3:00 AM. That had been a little over 13 hours ago. His legs were heavy and stiff as he shifted his weight in the cockpit.

Dave felt himself growing drowsy and reached for a stick of gum to help keep him awake. While the view through the windshield and right window was clear, he noted the dark clouds bubbling up on the southern horizon to his left. He would just make it to Tucson before the storm hit, he thought with relief. He was eager to see his sister, a sophomore at the U of A. His dad had promised to take them out to a really cool restaurant that night.

The sun was still high in the west, directly in front of him and the light temporarily blinded him. He didn't see the turkey buzzard swoop down to challenge the big red bird that had violated its domain.

"Shit!" Dave bellowed as the buzzard smashed itself to death on the windshield of the Taylorcraft with a loud thud. The small plane rocked violently. He took a deep breath and tried to recover. The cockpit was darkened by the blood and guts covering the windshield. He tightened his grip on the yoke and made himself scan the instrument panel again.

Check the controls, he told himself. He was reassured. Everything appeared normal. Well, you're still flying, blind as a bat, but still flying, he thought. Just then, the radio crackled, reminding him of the outside world. "Pick up the mike." He mumbled.

"Mayday! Mayday!" Dave broadcast the international distress call. Even as he calmed down, he began to realize the seriousness of the situation. He brought the plane back on a heading that, with luck, would get him back to the airport and his waiting father. God, don't let me crash, he thought. "Mayday! Mayday!"

Jim heard the faint Mayday between transmissions of the aircraft in the touch and go pattern. "Go ahead Mayday," he said evenly, screening the urgency he felt from his voice and trusting the other pilots to stay off the radio. Jake was immediately at his side, assessing the traffic situation and beginning a litany of contingencies in his head.

"This is ...Eight four eight Charlie. I hit something and can't see a damn thing out of the cockpit," the speaker responded.

"Eight four eight Charlie, say position, heading and altitude," Jim quickly replied.

"That's Duke Winter's plane." Jake recognized the call letters. Duke was well known in local flying circles, as he spent part of the year in Tucson and part overseeing his Harley shop in Daytona Beach. That way he could spend time with both of his kids.

Jake wrote down the response, glancing up to the BRITE, looking for the target.

Jake instructed, "Jim, clear the traffic pattern and have the pilots standby with approach control till advised."

Fred, grasping the situation, called the radar facility to apprise them of the event unfolding.

Jake turned to Jim. "If you want, I'll take over since I'm the pilot here," He knew that Jim, like most controllers, was not a pilot and this had the makings of an in the cockpit situation. Jim waved Jake to the local position and Jake plugged in.

"November forty-eight forty-eight C, this is Tucson, say type aircraft," Jake said.

"Taylorcraft."

"Roger, is that you, Duke?" He decided to slip into plain English.

"No. This is his son, Dave."

"This is Jake Morrow, are you OK?"

"I'm OK, but the windshield's splattered with blood and I can't see a thing." Dave paused. "Jake, my dad's meeting me at the airport. If anything happens, will you ...?"

"Don't worry, son. I've had plenty of stick time. We'll get you in. I have you on radar. Your heading and altitude are good for now. I'll be issuing new heading and altitude instructions as you get closer in."

Jake turned to Fred. "Page Duke Winters at the terminal and get him up here right now."

A few short minutes later Duke was standing next

to Jake. He grasped the situation at once. He stood ready to help in any way he could.

"November forty-eight forty-eight. How are you doing?" Jake asked.

"Not so good. My fingers are numb. I think there's something wrong. I can't get enough air." He sounded like he was gasping for breath.

"Dave," Jake lowered his voice. "Do you have a paper bag in the cabin with you?"

Dave looked around. "Yes, sir. My lunch bag."

"Great. Dave, take the bag and breath into it."

"What?"

"Breath into the bag. Keep it over your nose and mouth. Trust me on this, son." Jake insisted, sensing his resistance.

Dave emptied the bag. He could hardly move his fingers and now his arms felt weak. He put the bag over his face with one hand and started to breath.

"Now slow the breathing down, son."

Dave Winters slowly exhaled. He felt a connection with Jake's voice on the radio. He suddenly believed the man would get him in safely. He listened carefully for directions and for once in his life did everything he was told.

"Son, how's it going."

"Better, thanks."

Jake turned to Winters, whose face was grey with worry. "Anxiety attack. He'll be fine."

"Now, Dave take a look out the side windows and tell me what you see." Jake wanted to give the young pilot some ground reference.

"I see a mountain range off to the south... and a higher range to my north."

"Good. You're right on track. You're almost home."

Within minutes, Dave had landed roughly but safely on the runway. Seeing the plane taxi on solid ground Winters leaned his head forward and closed his eyes briefly.

"I owe you, man. If there is anything I can do for you..." Duke said gratefully. He shook Jake's hand.

"Come on, Duke, no thanks necessary. That's what we're here for."

Chapter Four: Puzzles

Bill Lee had wanted to be an investigative journalist ever since he could remember. He felt it in his blood. To him, an assignment was like a puzzle with hundreds of small interlocking pieces. As a kid he had learned to start looking for relationships between a few pieces and not to sweat the big picture. He was convinced that if he acted as if everything would eventually fall into place, it would. Most people couldn't handle the ambiguity that Lee dealt with on a daily basis, but he thrived on it. There was no more thrilling moment for him than when he got a new assignment and faced the fact that nothing appeared to make any sense at all. In that moment, his brain tingled with possibilities, and he relished the experience. The hard work would come soon enough, the painstaking effort of documenting the connections between the countless seemingly unrelated facts.

He was in this early stage of happy confusion, having recently been assigned to cover the Department of Transportation for the Post, when he heard the news that Jim Martin, his former mentor, was holding a press conference within the hour. He wouldn't miss this for the world. In his mind, Martin was one of the few politicians in Washington who had the guts to tackle the tough issues. He smiled, remembering how Martin would try to persuade him to enter politics.

"Your country needs you, young man." He would look at him and let the pause weigh heavy on his prize student. The idea still tugged at him, after all these years. The man was persuasive, he remembered with admiration. This should be worth the effort, he thought as he headed across town.

Bill had been covering the Washington beat for the past few years so the basic turf was familiar to him. The press conference was about to get underway as he made his way through the handful of reporters. They had gathered to witness the latest salvo in the ongoing skirmish between the most powerful member of the House FAA oversight committee and the agency's smooth talkers. He saw Joe Rosen, from the FAA's public relations team, and sat next to him.

"Hey, Joe. How's it going?" Bill grinned at the perpetually grumpy man.

"Must be getting close to election time. Martin's trying to fill his coffers again." Rosen grumbled. In truth, Rosen couldn't stand the young congressman. He was always seeking the spotlight and seemed committed to self-aggrandizement. He also made Rosen's job a lot harder.

"I don't know. I think he's risking a lot more than he gains from the notoriety. I think he's got guts." Bill's compliment was calculated to fuel the ongoing debate between the two men. Just then the object of their debate started to speak.

"Just a brief statement today, ladies and gentlemen. As you all know, the common understanding of parts use in our industry, is that parts either meet or exceed specifications for the intended use. If they do not, they are illegal. Earlier this morning, the investigator general provided our subcommittee with evidence of wide ranging abuse of replacement parts for our airlines. The end result of this abuse is that many of our planes are flying with substandard parts. As you know, the stress factors on some of these small parts is tremendous. The specifications for each part have been determined by the agency after years of testing. I want to be clear about how serious this matter is. As you may know, airplanes are designed to distribute stress, to spread it out. But this strength is based on the integrity of the whole. The failure of a single part too often results in catastrophe." He paused and looked around the room.

"My fellow committee members do not agree with my taking this matter to the public, but I believe the American people are intelligent enough to want the truth. I believe they deserve the facts. Maybe they can pressure the FAA and the Congress to take action on this critical safety issue. Thank you." Representative Martin was ushered out by his aide and left the room immediately. There would be no questions today.

"The idiot! I swear he gets off on scaring the public!" Rosen was livid.

"If it's not true, you'd have a point. But if it is true, why do you guys deny it? Everybody knows your standard playbook, Joe. Deny, defend and deflect. It would be a nice change to get the straight facts for once.

"Hey. Indulge me, Joe." Bill took the empty pop can he had been drinking from and placed it on the floor. Then he stood on top of the empty can.

"What?" Rosen was irritated.

"A plane is just a big tin can, Joe. It's only so strong. It doesn't take much to create a disaster." Bill bent down and touched the straw to the empty can, which suddenly crumbled with a loud pop.

Rosen looked startled. He tried to ignore the persuasiveness of the demonstration.

"This is Washington, Bill. Tell me one agency, one department that doesn't play by the same rules. They wouldn't last a day if they didn't. And besides, the agency is doing everything it can. You know we've got the best safety record in the world. You know it, Bill." Rosen looked weary. It would be a rough few days for his department, but they'd ride it out. They always did.

Two days later, Bill was sitting back, feet up on his desk and admiring his first article on the new beat. It was only two paragraphs buried in a back page, but it was a start. He turned sideways and searched the On-line Newspaper Database. Apparently he was the only one to have covered it. There was his headline: Martin Reveals Bogus Parts Investigation. It still amazed him why minor stories got front page banner headlines, while issues like this, that could really affect the lives of thousands of readers, often never saw print.

The phone rang and he picked it up while reaching for an apple.

"Bill Lee." He took a large bite. It was a little green and his face scrunched up against the impending sour taste.

"Mr. Lee?"

"Yes, this is Lee." He chewed on the apple, trying to adjust to the bitterness.

"Mr. Lee, I read your article on the bogus parts investigation. I'd like to thank you for printing it."

"You're welcome. Who is this?"

"I can't say over the phone. But I..." The voice paused briefly. "I want to talk to you, confidentially, about a related problem in the FAA."

Lee took another bite. The nuts were starting to come out of the woodwork. A common problem for any reporter. Sorting them out from the solid sources was almost an art.

"What's the problem?"

"Aging aircraft. The agency isn't facing up to it. I think it's one of the major safety issues the FAA has to face in the next five years. But they're not. They're denying it."

"What's your source of information?"

"I've been an airworthiness inspector in the agency for fifteen years. And I'm not speaking for myself alone. Several of us are really concerned."

"Do you have any documentation?" Bill threw his

apple in the wastebasket and reached for his pencil.

"I've been collecting facts for the past two years. I have results of stress tests. Actual certification errors. Documented cases of penalties overridden by top officials. I could go on."

"Why did you pick me? Why not go to someone like Congressman Martin with this?" Bill was curious.

There was a pause. "The truth is, Martin advised me to call you. He already knows all this, but can't get anywhere through the proper channels."

Bill put the pencil down and leaned back, listening.

"The fact that you were interested in the bogus parts gave me hope. This is so intertwined that you can't cover one story without it leading into the other."

"Are you here in town? Where can I meet you?" His heart started to pound.

"I'm here until evening. I can meet you at 3:00 at the Vietnam Memorial. I'll be the guy with the large brown briefcase."

"What's your name?" Bill ventured.

"No names, Mr. Lee. I'm way out on a limb already. No names."

Bill got to the memorial early. It was a sunny day and he walked up and down in front of the memorial while waiting for his source to show. It moved him, even now. The reflection of the visitors in the polished stone gave a fleeting sense of life to the names of the dead inscribed there. He went to the fifth panel and counted down eleven lines, then ran his fingers left to right. There it was. William Lee, his uncle, his namesake. He felt the energy from the man slip into his fingers then course through his body. Then he saw his reflection in the panel. He imagined the face of his uncle the day he had sailed off to war. He hoped he would bring honor to him. He hoped he would be proud. He stepped back from the memorial, scratched his forehead in a camouflaged salute, and looked around.

"Mr. Lee?" The man came up behind him.

Bill turned around and saw a well built, anxious looking man of about 50 with gray-streaked hair and tired eyes.

"Yes."

"I can't stay very long. I just wanted to make sure this gets into your hands..." He handed Bill the briefcase. He paused, looking into Bill's almond shaped eyes. "I don't know how to put this. I don't have a handle on it yet... but there's something screwy going on in the agency. Something that relates to the aging aircraft, the bogus parts and the unreported ...incidents."

"What is it?" Bill asked. "What's going on?"

"When I first started, careers in the agency were like a pipeline. Promotions came from within. You didn't get to be a manager in Air Traffic, Airways Facilities or Flight Standards without coming up through the field with a solid reputation. Since the air traffic controllers strike all that seems to have changed. Now they bring people in from the outside. I don't know if it's an attempt to get women or minorities in management. I just don't know. By the way, I'm all for qualified people of any persuasion running the shop. But the SES, sorry, senior execs that they bring in now sometimes don't know the first thing about the area they're responsible for."

"I'd imagine that creates some feelings."

"But that's not the worst part. The few that do get promoted to the top from inside go away for high level training, and it's like they get a lobotomy. They're just not the same people who went away. If they didn't listen before they went, they listen even less when they get back. They talk about the importance of feedback, but they're not open to hearing feedback themselves. Instead they accuse us of not being team players or not thinking the FAA way. Hell, I used to think that meant doing the best by the American people. Now, I don't know what the hell's going on. But it's not the same agency."

"So you tried to bring this," Bill lifted the briefcase, "to their attention?"

"Sure did. But it ruined my career. Now I'm just marking time till I get out. It's like they shrivel you into nonexistence. Someone should form a whistleblowers anonymous club. It's like really bad science fiction." He laughed wistfully. "First, they label you a disgruntled employee. Then you're assigned to some desk doing nothing of significance, just when you could be your most productive."

"Why are you doing this, then? Why not just forget about it."

"Why?" He thought a minute. "For my kids. And for me. So that my life winds up meaning something. So that the price I've paid won't be wasted."

Chapter Five: The Guru

Soon after Jake moved to Tucson he began hanging around air shows. Pilots swapped hard-to-find parts along with colorful stories. Occasionally they bought or sold planes with histories older than the men that flew them. Jake came across a beat up WW II trainer, an AT-6 and invested his time, money and passion restoring it to pristine condition. In the process, he became intimate with every inch of the plane and somewhere along the way named her Divine Wind.

He trained, tested and was certified as an air traffic controller. His plane restoration had proven expensive and he welcomed the good pay. The work kept him involved with planes on a daily basis. He was soon an excellent controller and passed up more challenging locations to stay in Tucson .

Jake experienced what many highly skilled

controllers do at some point in their careers. He had to decide whether to continue his upward move from supervisor into the higher ranks of management or to turn down promotion.

There were pros and cons involved in the decision. On the one hand, there was significantly more money and benefits to consider. Ordinarily, a man would feel he owed it to his family to increase his income and status, and to his company to step up to bat. But Jake had no family to consider, and he wasn't one to be unduly influenced by other people's expectations. On the other hand, he could once again feel the same pull that had led him to enlist and then embrace the mission of the special forces, strategic insertion in hostile environments. Promotion would mean saying good bye to the daily activities he had grown to love and the challenges at which he had come to excel. Jake had discovered that making a difference mattered to him. Making a living wasn't enough.

His manager, hoping to influence his decision, had signed him up for training and notified Jake by phone that he would be attending a management seminar. A letter soon arrived describing the two-week training session. It stated that the opening evening would be dedicated to "Dressing for success," and participants were to bring their power outfits to the workshop. They were also to bring exercise clothes, a comfortable pillow, and a book by Nietsche called Beyond Good and Evil.

Jake's manager, Bob Jacobs, stopped by to see him after work, the day before he was scheduled to head for the seminar. They drove to a little pub on Fourth Avenue for beers.

"Jake, a word of advice. When you get to the seminar, just keep your head down and your mouth shut. Trust me on this one. Don't give them anything to latch onto, do you get my drift?"

Jake looked at him with curiosity. "Bob, have you ever known me to keep my head down and my mouth shut? Why the hell should I start now?"

"This training is different, Jake." Jacobs frowned. "But you were special forces, so it'll be a piece of cake for you. It's really like a psychological boot camp. I think if you see it that way, you'll find it easier to handle. This is how they weed out the ones that can't take it." His face showed concern. He knew Jake's independent, thoughtful nature, yet it was that very quality that he knew would make him an outstanding manager.

"What do you mean by 'it'?" Jake asked.

"It?" Bob looked at him thinking for a moment.

"Abuse, Jake. Abuse."

By the time Jake arrived at the FAA's Oklahoma Center for Nontechnical Training (CNT), he was feeling a little uneasy. His curiosity had been aroused by the discussion with Jacobs and he could feel himself moving into a moderate state of alert.

He registered and picked up the key to his assigned room. His roommate, a fellow he didn't know named Harry Peterson from the contracts office in DC, had already arrived and taken the bed nearest the window. Harry appeared nervous to Jake, who assumed that Harry shared the same foreboding about this workshop that was gripping him. As they shook hands and exchanged introductions, Harry lingered a moment, looking into Jake's eyes, as though he wanted to say something. But Harry went back to putting on his suit coat and tie. He was having some difficulty buttoning his collar.

"It's a little tight," he said apologetically. Harry looked at Jake dressed as always in slacks, shirt and cowboy boots. "Aren't you going to put on your 'power suit'?"

Jake smiled at him. "This is what I'm comfortable

in, Harry. I live in the desert, and as far as I'm concerned this is my power suit."

Harry contorted his face while making a slicing gesture like Jake's neck would be chopped off.

They walked down to the seminar room together. Chairs were already set up in a semicircle, facing two chairs side by side at the front. The other participants arrived one by one, found their name tags on the table in the back of the room and put them on. Jake recognized a few people, but most were strangers to him. The chatter grew to a buzz as individuals looked around, made small talk and laughed nervously. Suddenly the door opened and in came an attractive woman of about 45 and a strikingly handsome younger man. The group fell silent.

The woman sat very straight in her chair. She looked calmly around the room, meeting each participant's eyes. When someone did not look directly at her and meet her eyes, she waited until they did before she went on, each in turn. The silence was intense. Her eyes finally rested on the young man next to her. She looked into his eyes for a long moment, then turned to the group.

"Welcome," she said with a smile, pronouncing each syllable distinctly. "Welcome. My name is Dr. Elizabeth Caldwell — and you all know my assistant,

Dr. Andrew Maxwell." Silence.

Jake looked around, noticing that individuals either were looking intently at Dr. Caldwell or appeared to have developed a compelling fascination with their shoes.

"Welcome," Caldwell repeated. "You have, each of you, come here today, to this place, to this moment in time — to be well. The definition of well that we will use is to be in a way that is morally good." She got up, went to a flip chart and wrote the definition, underlining the significant words. "Who thinks they know what it means to be morally good?" More people appeared deeply engrossed in observing their feet. After a brief pause Caldwell continued. "Not one of you knows what it means? Does anyone here remember the question I just asked?" There was an absolute silence in the room.

Dr. Caldwell turned in the direction of a young woman across the circle from Jake. She was neatly dressed in a navy suit, nylons and navy heels and appeared deeply absorbed by something on the floor.

"Francine?" As Francine turned her head to face Dr. Caldwell, her dangling earrings flew out to either side and continued a brief pendulum swing as she stopped with her gaze on Caldwell..

"I'm sorry. I..." She stopped as Dr. Caldwell went

to the flip chart and wrote the words: "I am sorry."

"You will soon come to understand how significant words are," she explained to the group. "The first words a person utters are most significant. They signify the state of the person. Francine has just revealed to us that she is in the state of being sorry." Dr. Caldwell then spelled out "Francine = I am sorry" on the chart.

Looking at Francine intently, Caldwell snarled unexpectedly. "You are sorry. You're a sorry manager. A sorry woman."

Francine's face turned scarlet and her breath caught in her throat. "That's not what I meant."

"You told us you are sorry." Caldwell turned to the group "Who sees what she is doing?"

Bob, a well groomed manager in his mid-thirties raised his hand. "Yes, Bob," Caldwell invited.

"She's not in integrity. She's trying to blame you for what she said." Bob smiled nervously, sensing that his head could be next on the chopping block.

"Good. How many of you understand what Bob is saying?" Caldwell looked around as over half the hands in the room went up.

"Francine, come here and stand facing the group." Caldwell pointed to a line of masking tape on the floor in front of the room. She moved her chair toward the group so that she could see her target more clearly. "Andrew — please start the tape."

Jake was startled to note the video recorder to the rear of the room. Andrew turned it on and focused the lens on Francine, who looked suddenly smaller and quite alone facing her colleagues.

Caldwell studied her quietly then said "Francine. Do you remember what 'to be well' means?" Francine shook her head. "Look at the board next to you and read what it says."

"To be well means to be in a way that is morally good," she replied, reading the words.

"Correct, yet when I asked before who knows what it means to be morally good, you said 'I am sorry'."

"Well, yes, but what I meant was that I didn't hear the question," she pleaded.

"Francine! Cut the bullshit. You said 'I am sorry.' What are you sorry about?"

" I don't understand. This is ridiculous." Francine squirmed under the pressure.

"No," snarled Caldwell. "You are ridiculous. If you don't mean what you say, you're lying to us!" Looking around at the group, Caldwell said, "Why would she lie to us? I want each of you to look carefully, very carefully at Francine. What one word describes who you see. Start over here." She pointed to one side of the room. Participants called out their impressions.

"Weak."

"Timid."

"Liar."

"Evil."

"Confused."

"Afraid," said Harry.

It was Jake's turn. Everyone waited. "Sad," said Jake.

"Evil."

"We can see you, Francine. You can't hide from us. And you don't really want to, do you? By telling us 'I am sorry', you're saying that you want to tell us your secret. You're seeking forgiveness. What is it that you are sorry for, Francine?" Caldwell's voice had become soft, almost tender. She walked over to the trembling woman and stood in front of her.

Francine looked at her. Suddenly all she saw was the radiant face of Elizabeth Caldwell, her eyes shining with compassion and understanding. Francine began to sob. Dr. Caldwell raised her hand quickly, discouraging any would-be rescuers in the group from offering help. She repeated the question, more gently, taking the young woman's hand.

"What is it that you are sorry for, Francine?"

Francine's eyes filled with tears. She fell to her knees, covering her face with one hand. "I.... I had an abortion three weeks ago," she blurted out, her voice suddenly constricting, making her sound like a little girl. "My husband doesn't even know that I was pregnant. I never told him. He wanted to start a family so much. I couldn't tell him. I...I didn't want a baby right now. I'm in line for a promotion and a baby would have ruined everything." The young woman looked up at Dr. Caldwell, her eyes begging forgiveness.

"Good, Francine. Being honest is a beginning." She put her hand on Francine's head and stroked her hair gently. Turning to the group the doctor said, "Now share with Francine one word that symbolizes her new being."

"Brave"

"Grace"

"Hope"

"Goodness"

Jake did not respond. He was trying to understand why he felt such uneasiness deep in his gut. Trying to make sense of how such a deeply personal revelation would have a place in a management training workshop. It went against everything his common sense was screaming at him. Now on full alert, he was aware of the video camera in the back of the room and of the man operating it.

"Well, well. Elizabeth, look what we have here." Andrew Maxwell and Elizabeth Caldwell were sequestered in her room on the top floor of the training center. The television was set up for reviewing videos. Andrew had just fast forwarded the most recent tape, carefully labeled "Francine Monet - SES Candidate".

It was 11:30 at night and the group was taking their first 15 minute bathroom break of the evening. They would probably continue training until 2:00 or 2:30 a.m. this first session. Then the group would get up for a mile run at 7:00 in the morning.

The evening had gone well, so far. Thanks to input from Francine's line manager, they had known about her abortion. Apparently her only confidant, a fellow manager, had driven her to and from the procedure and had shared the information with her boss.

"It always helps a new group move along, when breakdowns or breakthroughs occur right from the beginning," Caldwell said with the hint of a smile.

In fact, they had management reports on almost every participant: Francine's abortion, Harry's nosing around contracting irregularities, Bob's closet homosexuality. Everyone but Jake. They needed to get a fix on Jake, discover his weak spots. Find the sore, whatever it turned out to be — and rub hard until it bled.

"Listen to what Harry says." Andrew rewound the tape, then replayed a section. "He calls out the word afraid, then Jake says sad." He hit the pause button, played the section over and laughed disdainfully. "Harry's very perceptive, he ought to be afraid."

Elizabeth Caldwell frowned imperceptibly, thinking to herself that sometimes Andrew enjoyed his dissections a little too much.

"So — Jake Morrow, you're sad. But what are you sad about," Caldwell mused out loud. She was intrigued by the rebel, dressed casually in spite of having been notified to show up in a power suit. Her curiosity was further aroused because she had nothing on him. He would probably be the only challenge in the group. Everyone else had already relinquished their independence, and she was growing bored with their passivity.

"You're itching to take him on, aren't you." Maxwell smiled, not needing to mention Jake's name.

"I know that gleam in your eyes. When — tonight?"

"No. The time isn't right yet. We won't take him tonight. He's nowhere near his breaking point, and that's rule #1 — Go for the breakdown when you're sure you can get it. We don't want anyone trying to play hero. No — let's go after Harry. He's fragile, out of shape and wound pretty tight. I promised Army we'd handle him and we might as well get it out of the way." She labeled a fresh tape, "Harry Peterson - Retired."

"Let me do Harry," Andrew's eyes moistened. Breaking people's spirit turned him on. He moved closer and put his hands on her knees. "Please, Elizabeth," he breathed, sliding his hands slowly up her thighs and under her skirt.

Caldwell, looked down at him and frowned. She did not like being manipulated. She preferred being the one in control. Maxwell forced her back onto the bed. The moist warmth of his breath through her panties broke her train of thought. Her resistance melted away in waves of pleasure.

Back in the main room, Andrew lost no time setting up the video and preparing for Harry. He returned to his seat at the front of the room next to

Caldwell and looked slowly around at the different participants. Bob was smoothing his right eyebrow with his right hand. Francine crossed her legs and arms. Harry loosened his tie and undid the top button of his collar.

"Harry, you're next. Come up to the front and face the group," insisted Maxwell.

Harry complied, shooting a quick glance over at Jake.

"Why do you look to Jake? Do you expect him to rescue you?" Maxwell demanded.

"I.... I didn't know I looked at him," Harry mumbled.

"You know, Harry — I believe you. I believe you didn't know. I believe that you don't even have a clue. You just don't get it — do you?" He looked around to the group. "Who can see that Harry is unconscious — that he just doesn't get it?" Several hands went up.

Harry took out a handkerchief and wiped the sweat from his forehead. He didn't feel very good. The controlled diet at CNT was severe, and he was suffering from caffeine withdrawal. His head was pounding. The light was behind Andrew, and Harry could hardly make out his features. Blurred impressions of teeth and cold blue eyes combined with words he didn't understand. He felt oddly nauseated, like he had when, as a kid, he had been put to sleep with ether to have his tonsils removed. Once again he longed to go under, and go away. When Harry Peterson was finally told to return to his place, it could have been two minutes or two hours later.

It was 2:45 a.m. The group sat gazing around blankly, some in awe, some in terror and all exhausted. Caldwell looked slowly around the room. All night Caldwell had ignored Jake's boots, earrings and long brown hair, but she needed to begin gathering information for the inevitable confrontation.

"Tomorrow morning, you will all meet in front of the building promptly at 7:00 a.m. dressed to run. Then after breakfast, you will return to this room again dressed in your power outfits. Is that clear, Cowboy?" Dr. Caldwell questioned, laughingly looking at Jake. There were some titters.

"Quite clear, Liz," retorted Jake. The titters halted abruptly.

Dr. Caldwell frowned, "My name is Elizabeth."

Through his mounting tension Jake nodded slightly. "Quite clear, Elizabeth — My name is Jake."

Within twenty minutes, the exhausted participants had completed their brief toiletries and had bedded down for the promised relief of a few hours of sleep. But Harry couldn't sleep. He took out a small penlight and opened the briefcase that over the years had become a part of his attire. He clicked the light off as Jake rolled over. There was nothing to worry about. Jake was fast asleep. Harry once again opened his briefcase and took out a manila envelope. The contents of that envelope had become a weight around his heart. He wanted to do the right thing with it. He wanted to be morally brave. He carried it around with him, waiting.

But after his experience with Maxwell, Harry couldn't hold on any more. He needed someone to shift the burden to. He needed someone else to be heroic. It wasn't going to be him. He looked over at Jake, breathing slowly, peacefully. Harry felt ashamed for what he was about to do. He also felt hope.

At precisely 7:00 a.m. Jake and the other participants met in front of CNT dressed in running clothes. At 7:05 Dr. Caldwell and Andrew joined them and began to lead some stretching and warm-up exercises, and then pointed out the layout of the course.

"Now, I want you to listen very carefully to what I

am going to say. You don't have a clue what well being is. You are unconscious. You are undisciplined, lazy and gutless. You always take the easy way out. You have forgotten how to pursue your dream. How to push yourself beyond your limits. You are the one responsible for setting your limits too low. You are the only one limiting yourself."

Dr. Caldwell continued in inspired tones. "You are going to run a mile. Let it be the first mile of your life. Let your life begin right now. Today is different. Today, don't listen to your weakness. Don't give in to your body when it tells you to stop. When your body tells you it's tired, that's exactly the moment to dig deep inside and push. Push past your weakness. Push past your fear. Of course, you'll be afraid. You're afraid of greatness. Afraid of being all that you can be. In that moment, when you think you can't go on — I want you to hear only my voice, telling you to push through it. Discover you can do it."

She paused and looked at each participant. "Let the race begin!"

Jake was used to an early morning run so he took off, checking his watch and pacing himself. A few of the younger men initially sprinted past him but soon dropped back. Jake was alone and lost in the joy of the run. He never saw what was unfolding behind him.

About a third of the way into the run Harry Peterson, plodding along in last place, clutched his chest and fell to one knee gasping for breath. After a few seconds, he got to his feet and made another attempt to run. His pulse was going crazy and his eyes refused to focus.

Jake completed the half-mile and turned back toward the starting point. A few moments later, about 100 feet away from him, he saw Harry fall. Jake ran to him and took his pulse. Moments ago it had been racing wildly, but now it was almost impossible to detect.

"Call an ambulance!" Jake shouted to Francine who was nearby. Where are Caldwell and Andrew, he wondered. He stripped off his shirt, raised Harry's head slightly and rested it on the sweaty bundle. Harry looked up at him and grabbed his hand. He wanted to say something. Jake bent his head so he could hear.

Harry coughed weakly. "I.G. Only I.G..."

It took five minutes for the ambulance to arrive, and another five to administer CPR and get Harry on board. He died seven minutes later en route to the hospital with Jake at his side. Jake hung around until someone from security at the Center arrived at the hospital to answer questions and make arrangements, then he took a shuttle back to the Center.

On the way he tried to sort out his feelings. He was upset over the death of someone who he had started to befriend. He wondered if Harry had family and how getting the news to them would be handled. He suspected that if those who operated the Center had been trained by Caldwell and Maxwell compassion was not one of their prized values. The more he thought, the more he realized that it wasn't just Harry's death that disturbed him. He was deeply troubled by the oppressive training style, and he didn't relish finding himself right in the middle of it. He asked himself what it was that he found so disturbing. He had experienced harsher, more demanding training in the military, but he could not remember another circumstance where he felt his personal integrity had been so directly threatened.

As he analyzed his situation he began to see that Caldwell and Maxwell had set the context so that he and the other participants were left with only two fundamental choices. They could comply and give up their right to self determination — or they could refuse to comply and be rejected as unacceptable training material. They would be labeled as lacking commitment to FAA values, as not being team players. It followed they would also be rejected by the FAA as unfit for promotion, possibly not worthy of being a part of the FAA in any capacity.

Neither choice was acceptable to him. Jake realized he was about to step across a line from which there was no return. As long as Caldwell and Maxwell set the terms of engagement, there was no way to win. He would at best be a loser in his own eyes, and at worst he would be seen as a traitor. He felt a heaviness settle over him. Somewhere on the ride back he decided that his personal integrity was more valuable to him than even his career with the FAA. He could not continue to let Caldwell and Maxwell define his world view. If this was a battle over who sets the context, then his only recourse was to broaden the field, to wage the war on his terms. He needed to persuade someone in authority that the training they were promoting could destroy the capacity for independent thinking in an agency that relied on that very quality to fulfill its mission.

On his return to CNT, Jake went directly to his room and packed his bags. He needed time and distance to think things through. By 2:30 p.m. Jake Morrow was on a plane heading back to Tucson. He had not noticed the plain manila envelope that Harry had slipped into his suitcase early that morning.

Chapter Six: The Dilemma

Dani smiled as she looked over her shoulder. She was pouring hot water for tea into two cups. In some ways, she thought not much had changed in ten years. She was still in her tiny efficiency, although she had fixed it up and it was quite charming. Bill Lee, now an investigative reporter for the Post, was still her neighbor and best friend. She had finally made it through law school, had interned with the Government Accountability Project for a few years and had in recent months found a job with the FAA.

Her smile broadened as she remembered the first time she had heard Bill trying to impress a girl. He was a skilled classical guitarist, and to create the right mood he'd toss off a passionate flamenco. During the evening, the strains coming down the hallway would build into an ever mounting crescendo, then there would be silence. The look of contentment on his face the next day was evidence of his success. She shook her head as she recalled that on the few occasions he had struck out, he'd invited a few of his friends from the international students' club at the university over. They would invariably chant Gregorian dirges for hours and get drunk on red wine. In actuality, these nights were few and far between. Bill, with his tall, angular body, cultured French/Japanese accent and handsome face, didn't step up to bat all that often, but when he did he was almost always a hit with women.

He was also a third degree black belt in karate and had encouraged Dani to take classes. He admonished her that it was essential for a woman alone in D.C. to be able to protect herself. She had gone to the dojo that he had recommended, and found herself loving the Zen like forms and two hour workouts. She still visited the dojo when she could and had maintained her skill level.

Through the years their relationship was structured almost completely around the game of chess. It had been years before Dani had given Bill even the hint of a challenge. Eventually an occasional game lasted for days, interspersed with work assignments, tea and philosophical conversations. On rare occasions, though Bill never suspected the intensity of her satisfaction, she won. They were now in the middle of a game and had taken a break for tea. Bill reached into the canvas tote that he carried with him everywhere and pulled out a small box of chocolates.

"This is to celebrate your new promotion — to the manager in our midst." He smiled, raising the box in a toast, his eyes twinkling at her over the top of his glasses.

Dani opened the wrapper, took off the cover and passed her index finger slowly over each delectable. She carefully selected a chocolate-covered raspberry jelly. The years had been kind to her. Her long, shiny brown hair was loosely gathered into a thick French braid resting against the nape of her neck. Her complexion was clear and unlined. She wore no makeup, and others would find it difficult to decide if she was in her twenties or thirties. When not at work she lived in jeans and sloppy sweaters. Although not striking, Dani was serenely beautiful. She smiled and nodded acknowledgment to Bill as she bit into the morsel.

"So when do you move into your new office?"

"This Monday. I still can't believe it. You know they passed over several people that I felt were more qualified and had more experience in the agency than me. I still feel a little uncomfortable about the whole thing." Dani had been selected to head the team of investigators in the acquisitions department, a major coup for someone so new to the FAA.

"What is it that you feel uncomfortable about?"

"Nothing, really. I'm just feeling grateful, I guess. You know, it's just about ten years — and we've been through so much. I'm just glad you're my friend." She sighed and smiled slightly. While they had never been lovers, Dani loved him. His enthusiasm and curiosity were refreshing and increasingly rare in the growing cynicism of her world. He had helped her with research during law school and encouraged her when she had been tempted to give up. He was in every way her best friend.

Bill raised his eyebrows. "Something's on your mind. What is it?" he coaxed.

"You know, when I was thinking about leaving the convent, I was really afraid. I didn't know who I was. I felt like an amoeba that would sort of just ooze out and lose its shape without the structure of the convent to maintain it. I wondered if there was a real person underneath the nun. What were my values? I didn't even know if I believed in God. Was it the nun that believed? If so — did I? So I went to see Father Bernard and asked him for some advice."

"You mean the Jesuit?" Bill recalled the name from some class at Georgetown.

"Yes. Well, he told me that I would go through a

transition — like a butterfly does. I'd be growing up, even though I thought I was already mature. He suggested that I put a parenthesis around my core beliefs."

"A parenthesis?"

"Yes. Like putting jewels in a safe in your home. You keep them close at hand so that you can take them out and use them any time you need to. He said that this was my time to experiment. I could look at the world with new eyes — my eyes, and let myself know what I saw. Then, when I felt ready, I'd choose my own values, old or new. He told me that I would always have the option of re-choosing and not to be afraid." Dani was thoughtfully silent for a moment.

"Well? What was the result of your experiment?" Bill looked at her quizzically.

"I think most people are afraid of letting themselves know what they really see about the way the world is. It's easier to take somebody else's view and be part of the group. Anyway, here I am moving up in the FAA. I've got a great new promotion and the kind of job I love, analyzing, investigating. I ought to be delighted, but I feel unsettled."

"I suspect that every organization has its own culture. Its own set of values. So does the FAA. Are you afraid of losing yourself in it, the way you did in the convent — and not finding your way back?" They sat together a moment in silence.

"By the way, what ever happened to Father Bernard?"

Dani grinned. "Married with two kids," she replied.

~

That same day John O'Meara, of the Southwest Region of the D.O.T. Investigator General's office was meeting with his immediate supervisor.

"Ed." He handed a thin file to his boss. "I'm not sure what way to go with this complaint. It's from some controller in Tucson who went to a management training seminar run by Dr. Caldwell. This is the fourth complaint of its kind within the last six months. What should I do with it?"

His supervisor, a thin, balding man with a perpetual, insincere smile, reassured him. "John, this is just a philosophical difference about training methods. We've had to deal with this type of complaint for years. First we had T-groups, then encounter groups. Now you've got all the step programs. Some people like 'em, some hate 'em. Hell, they've had to drag some guys kicking and screaming to these things.

Especially the jerks. You know, guys afraid of any change. Dinosaurs. Anyway they're all just fads, as far as I'm concerned. Training is training and it's not in our jurisdiction."

"This Caldwell sounds like a kook, Ed. Are you sure we shouldn't look into it? I mean, doesn't some of this stuff sound bizarre?"

"It's Jake Morrow who's bizarre. He's a cowboy, John. You know the type, a smart-ass controller."

John darted a quick glance at his boss. He had never mentioned Jake's name.

Ed continued. "Hey, I know guys who've been through Caldwell's workshops. Sure she cuts to the quick, even spills some blood and brags about it — but she gets people in line. Shape up or ship out, I say. Hell, some people swear she's saved their lives. They worship her. For every one who complains, there's ten who feel she's the best thing that ever happened to them. I tell you what. Let me handle this for you. I know what to do with it."

After John left his office, Ed reached for the phone and dialed long distance. When the other party answered he said. "You were right. Morrow is a risk. Keep an eye on him. I'll sit on the complaint at this end. In the meantime, I think I'll recommend John O'Meara gets some management training." Ed's perpetual smile broadened momentarily, but his eyes were cold.

~

It was lunch time in the nation's capital. In front of FAA headquarters a broad-shouldered man with a pit bull neck came out of the building. He squinted in the bright sunlight, then strode over to one of the many street vendors in the area who catered to the working crowd. He ordered a hot dog and root beer. Biting off a third of the hot dog, Joseph Army, the acting head of operations for the FAA, turned and strolled casually down Independence Avenue. As he reached the corner, he was joined by a tall young man with sun-drenched blond hair and observant eyes. For a moment, neither acknowledged the other. They continued a few moments walking together in step.

Army dropped the rest of his lunch into a sidewalk trash can and looking straight ahead said, "Well, Andrew. Will we stay on schedule in spite of the new administration? God knows who they'll put in charge of the agency or the DOT."

"Yes, sir. There's great interest in Caldwell's training in the DOT, even the DC IG's office has requested a seminar. We're on schedule to move into the NTSB next month. And there's very good news from the recent election, sir." He paused, enjoying jerking Army's chain, making him wonder.

"It seems," he said, quickly picking up the irritation in Army's frown, "that our new Vice President is a fan of Caldwell's from some workshop he attended a few years back. He's put out inquiries about Caldwell giving a presentation to the Council."

Army sucked in his breath sharply. "Damn. Who would have guessed? So all this talk about reinventing government and downsizing is really...... Well."

Andrew smiled. He knew he had surprised Army, a rare and delicious occurrence.

"What about our man in security. Is he secure yet?"

"Almost, sir. Still has to work out some problems in his marriage. He's scheduled for the couples seminar. That should reel him in." Andrew's voice was somewhat tentative. "Damn fool. He's got a cock for a brain. But he's loyal, and he worships Caldwell. Elizabeth got him off the sauce and saved his career. I figure he'll do what he's told."

"I hope you're right. The weakest link and all." Army's eyes narrowed as he glanced at Andrew Maxwell. The man's a snake, he thought. Absolutely invisible. He had two graduate degrees, was a certified genius, and was one of the few men in Washington who made Joseph Army uneasy. "We'll meet again the next time you're in town." With a slight wave of his hand he dismissed Andrew Maxwell, the new deputy director of FAA training.

Joe Army had himself avoided attending Caldwell's sessions. He recognized the powerful grip she was exerting over the agency and he didn't like it. Who knew what her agenda really was? He vowed to neutralize Elizabeth Caldwell once his own ambitions were secured. But in the meantime, it was to his advantage to keep Maxwell in close contact with her. That way he could learn her methods as well as the extent of her contacts. More troublesome to him than Caldwell was the thought that one day he might have to deal with Andrew Maxwell.

Chapter Seven: The Coal Miner's Canary

Six months had passed since Jake's request for an investigation into the training methods of Dr. Elizabeth Caldwell. John O'Meara had made it quite clear that his office viewed the matter as a philosophical difference over training methods, and as such it fell outside the jurisdiction of the Southwest Investigator General's Office. Since then a lot had happened. Jake had been taken off tower duty and given a supervisory job pushing papers in one of the back offices of the FAA at the Tucson airport. It was a lateral move, his pay and grade were the same. He was still a first level manager, but he had been marginalized and he knew it.

The most disconcerting aspect of the situation, was that nothing was ever said. Little things just started happening. Friends began avoiding his eyes. They forgot to invite him out for drinks after work. He began to feel invisible, like a social leper.

Jake's boss, Bob was polite but distant when he

went in for his midyear performance review, until he shut the door behind him.

"What the hell did you say to Caldwell?" Bob roared. He really had liked Jake. He had promoted him first as supervisor, then as first level manager. "I tried to get you into the next training class, so you could complete it and move on, but Caldwell wouldn't let you in. I've never heard of them keeping someone out before. You know that Caldwell's approval is needed for anyone to move up in the FAA. You've cut you own throat, Jake. I warned you. Why didn't you listen? Now my boss is insisting that you're roadkill. He wants you out."

"Bob, something very wrong is going on in the FAA — and you know it. Level with me. Who the hell is this Caldwell, and what is her hold on the agency?" Jake looked his friend and mentor straight in the eyes, forcing him to respond.

Bob walked over to the radio on his file cabinet. He turned it on to a raucous channel, came back and sat down facing Jake.

"I don't know what's going on. All I know is that Caldwell is probably more powerful than the administrator. And I also know that as long as you bend over, jump through the hoops, they do leave you alone." Bob lowered his voice. "She seems to have eyes everywhere."

"What's going on is criminal, Bob." Jake ignored the implied danger. "They're brainwashing people. I think they would stop at nothing. What I saw going on was a brutal form of psychotherapy, getting managers to confess personal sins in front of their peers and videotaping the whole damn thing. How has Caldwell gotten so involved in the hiring and firing process anyway? This mess stinks and something needs to be done about it."

"What do you have in mind?" Bob asked. He knew that he would feel the repercussions of any action that Jake took, and his career also would be on the line.

"I've already tried the local IG and regional administrators, but they claim this is out of their jurisdiction. How far up do you think this goes?" Jake noticed Bob's eyes drift over to the picture of his family on his desk. He knew instinctively that he could not count on Bob.

"Well, let's face it, Caldwell's been training the senior execs for over eight years. So that means someone at the top likes what she's up to, otherwise she would have been out a long time ago. I think they're pleased with the results — even if the methods are weird."

"Well, I've come to the conclusion that silence is what keeps this thing alive. You know, Bob, I'm about as powerful as a coal miner's canary."

Bob looked at Jake questioningly. "What do you mean?"

"Like the canaries that coal miners brought with them into the mines to detect dangerous gases. If the canaries died, the miners knew the situation was life threatening." Jake looked at his friend sadly. "Keep your eyes and ears open, Bob. It looks like there's only one way to find out how insidious this thing really is."

Bob sat alone at his desk after Jake left. He turned the radio off and looked at the picture of his family for a long while. He rubbed his forehead with his fingertips several times, then quickly reached into a file folder in his drawer. He took out the papers and laid them on his desk. Bob rolled his head back and stretched his neck to the left and right. Then he wrote Jake's name on the termination papers.

~

Dani sat staring at the clock outside Joseph Army's office. His secretary, Ana Estefan, was a fixture in the place. She had worked her way up from the secretarial pool to the highest level an executive secretary could reach. She had done this by being efficient, accurate, treating people fairly and keeping her mouth shut. She picked up the intercom and nodded. Hanging up, she turned to Dani and smiled.

"Mr. Army will see you now."

Dani thanked her and went in. Army's request for a meeting had been unexpected and she wondered what it was about. He gestured to two chairs off to the side of his desk and joined her there.

"Thanks for coming, Ms. O'Malley. And by the way, congratulations on your recent promotion." Unknown to her, Army had played a large part in her advancement, wanting to put in place people who weren't already indebted to political rivals. He needed allies he could mold to his own particular world view.

"Thank you, sir. Delighted to finally meet you. Please call me Dani." Dani held out her hand and Army shook it warmly.

"Well, let's get right to it, Dani. The administrator has recently received a formal letter of complaint from a former ATC manager in Tucson about the training methods of Dr. Elizabeth Caldwell. Now, there's nothing unusual in complaints about training. Most people fight change, as you know. Almost every new management training program gets complaints from someone. We had no reason to think anything would be different in this case. But this Morrow is turning out to be a potential troublemaker. He claims to have documented proof of contracting irregularities. It's time for us to take a good look at his complaint and find out what documentation, if any, he has. I would like you to go to Tucson very quietly and look into the matter. Report back to me on what you find."

"What is the agency's position on Caldwell?" Dani was curious. She had heard vague rumors about her training.

"Do you know anything about horses, Dani?" Army smiled when she shook her head. "Well, I grew up on a farm. I guess that makes me an expert, right? Horses get so attached to their stall that if the barn burns down, they'll die rather than leave a familiar place. People are more like horses than we care to admit. Caldwell represents change. That's why there are such strong reactions to her training. Some people love it, others absolutely hate it, but the reality is that things change, and we as an agency better get used to that fact."

"What about Morrow? Where will I find him?"

"He's been fired for insubordination, but we hear he's still in the Tucson area. Check with his former boss, Bob Jacobs. He'll point you in the right direction."

It hadn't been difficult to locate Jake, once Dani arrived in Tucson. Bob Jacob's voice sounded concerned as he suggested she try the Southwest School of Aviation, next to the Tucson airport. He had heard that Jake had found work there as a flight instructor. She called the school and finally connected with Jake, and they arranged to meet that afternoon at a restaurant called the Blue Willow.

As Dani slid into her rented car and drove up Campbell Avenue from downtown Tucson, the desert started to have its way with her. It was unseasonably hot for late April, and the afternoon sun had baked the city streets until she felt like she was in a dry sauna. She opened the car windows and turned off the air conditioner, eager to experience this strange environment that seemed both harsh and sensuous. Haunting and unfamiliar smells, like a heady sweet musk of orange blossoms and honeysuckle, invaded her senses. Every few blocks, as she passed a palo verde or mesquite tree, the desert birds, mostly cactus wrens, grackles and sparrows, chirped enthusiastically, blending oddly with a medley of traffic sounds.

Dani had never been out of the northeast, except for her brief visit to LAX. Life in D.C. was structured and busy. The pace in the desert was certainly slower. She noted that in spite of the lack of bright green vegetation, there were strange looking, brownish-green plants everywhere. Cactus of all shapes clawed for survival out of small openings of cracked earth. Little beads of sweat tried to form on her face and arms, but evaporated almost immediately. Someone at the hotel had told her that the desert was so dry, you could get shivers getting out of a pool at 110°. She noticed that she was driving below the speed limit and smiled. She felt unusually relaxed and wished that she had taken an afternoon siesta.

The Blue Willow was a small, white building, accented with seventies looking dark blue swirls of paint that distinguished it from its Santa Fe style neighbors. The building was surrounded by mesquite, palo verde and its namesake willow trees. Dani opened the front door and stepped into another world, far removed from Beltway timeclocks and tasks. Beyond the dark entry way and bar she saw a large, open courtyard with a brick floor. Tables were shaded by trees and above there was blue sky everywhere. The style was casual and quaint and definitely Southwest. Dani mentioned to the hostess that she was there to meet a Mr. Morrow.

The girl looked her up and down somewhat resentfully and then said matter of factly, "This way, please." She led the way around the courtyard to a secluded table in the shade and pulled out a chair. There, nursing a Corona with a lime wedge in the bottle, was Jake Morrow.

Jake was not quite what Dani had expected. The FAA Washington types she knew were for the most part clean cut with a professional air about them. The man standing in front of her, hand held out in greeting, wore boots, jeans and a white cotton shirt with rolled up sleeves. His unruly brown hair was pulled back behind his neck. The sun played on his face as he stood there, dancing patterns of light and shade filtered by the palo verde branches above. Dani noticed the light flickering on the hairs of his chest and in the blue of his eyes and felt a strange tightness in her stomach. She cleared her throat unconsciously, extended her hand and smiled.

"Very nice to meet you, Mr. Morrow. I'm Danielle O'Malley. Please call me Dani."

A few hours of intense conversation and note

taking passed. The waiters moved silently from table to table with long matches, lighting candles and standing lanterns, as the desert sky turned from blue to orange pink, mauve and finally a deep, dark blue. Other customers had come and gone and the arrival of the latest group announced that the evening dinner hour had begun. Dani finally placed her pen on top of the notepad and leaned back, signaling the end of the formal investigation for the day.

"What's your personal opinion of Caldwell?" Jake inquired, watching Dani closely. She had seemed open and fair-minded in her questions so far.

Dani stirred the ice in her tea thoughtfully. "I haven't formed a personal opinion yet. But I'm very curious. Never having met the woman, everything is hearsay. But I am fascinated by the strong reactions people seem to have to her. It seems that people either love her almost to the point of adoration, say she's changed their lives — or they despise her, as though she's evil personified. No one seems in between, indifferent. Back in Washington, the criticisms are all whispered. Those who dislike her are afraid to speak out publicly. Until today, I'd been toying with the theory that her training was too challenging for some, a kind of hazing ritual that required a certain strength of character to get through."

"What happened to change that?" Jake asked playfully.

"Well." Dani smiled. "Today I met you."

"And?"

"And, now I'm developing a new theory." Dani looked at Jake with the hint of a twinkle in her eyes. "I think that people who have problems with authority might also rebel against Caldwell's strong-arm tactics."

Jake looked at her closely. Her hair, softly pulled back from her face lent a hint of severity to her appearance, yet she radiated a gentle beauty that touched him. She wasn't cold or remote, yet he found himself searching for something in this woman. Something seemed missing. At that moment Dani looked directly into his eyes and smiled. It was the open smile of a child and his heart was captivated. In that moment he understood. She had not yet been fully wakened.

Chapter Eight: The Anniversary

After the interview with Jake, Dani met with several managers in the region. Most of them expressed enthusiasm about Caldwell's training and how it had impacted their lives, although they were vague when she asked them to be specific about its effect. They used vague words like "incredible", "transformational" and "breakthroughs" to describe their experiences. One woman however, an upper level manager from Phoenix, extracted a promise of confidentiality.

"If you mention my name, I'll deny ever talking to you," she had threatened. But then, hesitantly, she opened up. "I was attending a week long retreat for women executives in the FAA, a program that my manager assured me I needed in order to get ahead in the agency. Then, out of the blue, Caldwell ridiculed and harassed me for close to five hours straight." She paused as she remembered the experience and a visible shiver went down her body. She frowned and continued.

"One of the exercises was..." She paused and looked at Dani, as if to verify it was safe to continue. "Was to stand before Caldwell, Maxwell and the rest of the group in panties and bra. As you can see, I'm overweight. My size is a sensitive subject for me. It was bad enough to have to display myself to the other women, but I was mortified to have to stand in my underwear in front of Maxwell. Caldwell accused me of self-indulgence, of gluttony. Of not being a team player due to my selfish habits. When I didn't break, Maxwell started calling me names, screaming 'doughnut queen' and other abusive phrases." She looked shyly into Dani's eyes.

"I know it must sound ridiculous to you. Almost funny..." Her voice trailed off and her face twisted in discomfort. "But it wasn't funny to me at the time. Maxwell let me know in no uncertain terms that he found me disgusting. Well, they finally won. I broke."

Dani reached over and put her hand on the woman's slumping shoulders.

"Why did you stay?" Dani asked. "Why didn't you just walk out?"

"No one walks out, not if they value their career in the FAA. You either take it or kiss your career goodbye. You know, they never even explored my medical history. I tried to tell her about my recent thyroid radiation treatment and she accused me of 'victim speak.'"

Late that night before she left Tucson, the phone rang in Dani's hotel room. As she picked up the receiver, she heard a somewhat muffled, masculine voice.

"I hear you're investigating Caldwell's training."

"Who are you?" she asked. "What do you want?"

"What they did to Jake is criminal. But it's just the tip of the iceberg." The voice on the other end of the phone paused a minute. "If I'm right, young lady, and if you're doing an honest, thorough investigation — watch your back. This thing is bigger than you realize, bigger than anybody in the FAA realizes."

There was a gentle click and then silence.

Dani sat for a while thinking about what the caller meant, about who it might have been. Then she spread out the information she had gathered on the hotel bed and mulled it over. Looking through the materials, she noted copies of the contracting irregularities Harry Peterson had given to Jake, newspaper clippings referring to Caldwell's work with the IRS, as well as her own notes from the meeting with Jake and the other managers. Her gut told her that Jake was onto something. There was something seriously, perhaps even criminally wrong here. But Dani never acted on instinct. She had to see to believe.

Later that night, Dani lay awake for a long time. She had a hard time falling asleep, tossing and turning until she finally drifted off.

The nun was walking up and down the aisle, preparing the squirming class of seven year old girls for first communion. "How many gods are there?" she asked, turning and looking through the shy little girl. "One," she replied. "There is only one god." The nun nodded. "And how many persons are there in god?" The little girl looked at her. "There are three persons." The nun tested her. "And how many gods?" "There is god the father, then there is god the son and there is god the holy ghost." She replied, holding up three fingers. "There are three gods." The nun came closer and put her hand under the child's chin. "Listen to me very carefully. There is only one God. This is a

mystery, my child. It can only be understood by
those who have faith. True believers don't
question the church in matters of faith. Do you
understand?" As she spoke, the nun's hand slid
down to the girl's neck. Her breath caught in her
throat. She couldn't swallow or breath. "Do you
understand?" The nun repeated. The little girl
nodded in growing terror. She understood.

~

The following week, Dani was cleaning her
apartment when Bill rang the bell. She was relieved to
see him. He had been out of town on assignment
during her recent investigation. Usually, they would
sip tea and catch up on each others lives, but tonight
there was an earnestness about her as she took Bill's
hand and brought him over to the table. She pointed
to a large manila envelope lying there.

"I want you to hold onto this for me," she said.
They both sat down.

Bill looked at her questioningly. 'What's in it?" he
asked.

"You know the Caldwell case that I've been
looking into? This has a copy of the information I've

gathered so far. I want you to hold onto it for safe-keeping."

"This isn't like you, Dani. What's going on here?"

"I'm not sure. You know I went out to Tucson to meet with Jake Morrow?" She looked at him, to see if he remembered.

"Sure. How'd it go?"

"The interviews were fine. But since I've gotten back things just keep getting stranger by the day. I went in to present my oral briefing to Joseph Army. He sat there and nodded a lot. Then he told me not to bother with a written report, which is against department policy. When I questioned his decision, he said that he wanted me to go deeper into the investigation before I came to any conclusions. So as of tomorrow morning, I'm off to spend two weeks getting trained by one Dr. Elizabeth Caldwell."

"Can't you get out of it?" Bill felt protective. While he sensed a story, he hated that Dani's investigation was taking her right into the middle of it.

"I want to go — to see for myself what's going on. But I have this feeling there may be a lot at stake here."

"You could be at stake here, Dani. Don't do this to yourself. From what you've said, this Caldwell is pretty potent and very persuasive."

"Don't worry about me, Bill. I can take care of myself. At least I'm going in with my eyes wide open. I've taken enough psychology to know mind control when I see it. Don't forget that I spent seven years in the convent. When it comes to brainwashing, I was trained by the very best."

"I know, I know. It's just that, well... why did you give me that package?"

Dani looked over at the manila envelope and then back up at Bill. She just looked at him quietly, without saying anything.

~

Ana Estefan finished dialing the phone. "Is Dr. Caldwell available? Mr. Army would like to speak to her." She waited a moment. "Thank You. Please hold for Mr. Army."

"Sir," she pressed the intercom button for Army's office "I have Dr. Caldwell on the phone." Ana hung up. She noticed that the door to Army's office was slightly ajar. Picking up a file from her desk, she went over to the file cabinet nearest the door and listened. She picked up the conversation mid sentence.

" ....O'Malley...yes, our internal investigator...a

little too efficient for her own good... needs to have her corporate thinking fine tuned." Army paused and then continued. "Well, she spent seven years in a convent. As far as we can tell a real goody two shoes." Army laughed. "That's right. I remember you saying that. Flip over a person's greatest strength, and you'll find their greatest weakness. Two sides of the same coin. Well, see what you can do. I want her thinking the FAA way. I'll want the usual report. By the way, what have you learned about this character Jake?" He paused, listening to Caldwell. "I think you're right. He's a loner. Not part of any organized group. That keeps things simple."

As he hung up, Army looked up and noticed the door opened slightly. He moved toward it quickly, grabbed the knob and opened the door wide. Ana was busy at her computer. Army frowned with mild embarrassment. He shook his head, chuckled and went back to his desk.

~

It was late in the evening and Jake was at the bar in one of the many small but colorful establishments that populate the area around 4th Avenue in downtown Tucson. In uncharacteristic fashion he had downed three straight vodkas. A few couples sat at tables, and the bartender was splitting his time between Jake and two men in a quiet but heated conversation at the far end of the bar. He washed and dried each glass, then held it up to the light to check for streaks. All the while he listened. At the rear of the smoke filled room, under a hanging lamp that bathed him in a gentle light, sat a young man, singing and strumming accompaniment on his guitar. Jake was in a reflective mood. He ordered another vodka and turned to listen. Ordinarily he didn't pay much attention to the words in songs. But something in the singer's voice seared through his soul.

>if I believe in you, would you betray me?
>if I put my faith in you would you save me?
>are you real or are you fake?
>a creation of mankind or something great?
>can you show me the way?

>I'm feeling empty — I'm lost inside
>I've heard about you and how you died
>people say I should believe
>but I'm not one who's easily deceived
>do you believe in me?

> if I believe in you would you betray me?
> if I put my faith in you would you save me? *

For a moment, tears welled up in Jake's eyes, but he cleared his throat and belted down the remaining drink. The bartender looked at him.

"Troubles?"

Jake nodded.

"A woman?"

Jake looked up at the bartender a bit startled and nodded. He trusted him instinctively. He took out his wallet and removed a small, tattered picture that he could not recall ever sharing and held it up for this stranger to see. It was a picture of a lovely young woman, smiling quietly and holding a rose. There was a glow of happiness on her face.

Jake remembered the day. He had just bought a rose at the airport and asked her to marry him. She had said yes, and they had just enough time before his plane left to squeeze into a photomat and take a picture for each other to keep while they were apart.

"She's a beauty," the bartender said genuinely. He waited, letting Jake have his memories, knowing the story would be told when it was time.

** *Lyrics, if I believe, Jon Murphy, Tucson, copyright 1996*

"We had been married almost a year when I got called up on a special assignment. We had a two-month old baby girl." He looked up. "She begged me not to go. But I told her it was my duty." Jake could feel a lump rising in his throat. He swallowed. "There was a plane crash..." His voice trailed off and Jake looked up at the ceiling and with some difficulty swallowed again.

"I'm sorry."

Jake nodded. He looked up at the bartender and took a deep breath. "They didn't tell me until the mission was over. National security." His jaw muscles flexed and his voice conveyed controlled rage and grief as he continued. "I never got to say good-bye." Jake held up the picture. "This is all I have left." He looked at the picture once more and put it carefully back into his wallet. "Today would have been our 12th anniversary."

The bartender poured Jake another drink. "This one's on the house," he said.

Chapter Nine: The Disciple

Dani was one of twelve participants in the executive level training seminar being held in a huge beach house along one of North Carolina's barrier islands. The area was hauntingly beautiful. Although there were other beach houses off to the south, to the north along the shore a protected bird and sea turtle reserve guaranteed miles of privacy.

They had gathered in the large second floor living room. French doors opened onto a balcony that overlooked the dune and the ocean beyond. Dani had picked a seat so she could take in the view. She was for the moment lost in the plaintive sounds of gulls on the beach just yards away. Unconsciously, she inhaled deeply, and the smell of the salt water and dune grass filled her senses.

The group was engaged in small talk and grew quiet when Caldwell entered the room. She was smaller than Dani had expected, having anticipated a more imposing figure. This woman was slender with liquid hazel eyes. She spent the first twenty minutes getting acquainted with each participant. Caldwell looked attentively at each person as they introduced themselves, told what part of the FAA they were from and what they hoped to get from the training. As each finished she looked them in the eyes and welcomed them with a smile. Halfway through the introductions Dani noticed the man in the back of the room focusing a videocam on each person as they spoke.

Across the room sat a delicate young woman with a sweatshirt wrapped around her shoulders. Her name was Sharon. "I'm from evaluations." She smiled seductively. "And I'm cold," she said with a nervous little laugh."

"Why are you here, Sharon? What do you want to get out of the session?" Caldwell looked at her with some amusement.

"Well, I'm not sure. I'm here because my superior thought I needed more self-confidence." Sharon looked anxiously at Caldwell.

Caldwell smiled and welcomed her. Sharon breathed an audible sigh and her body visibly relaxed.

Next, was a big man of military bearing with salt and pepper hair.

"My name is Dave and I'm from Airway Facilities.

Frankly, I'm here because I was told to get my butt in gear."

"And what do you want?" Caldwell said gently.

"I'm at that point in my life where I need to think about what's really important to me. I'm here to rethink my values."

"Very good. Welcome, Dave."

Caldwell faced Dani when it was her turn and smiled expectantly. For a moment, Dani was at a loss for words. "My name is Dani O'Malley. I'm from Acquisitions." She paused and looked into Caldwell's eyes. "I'm here to see what's real about your training." Her heart pounded.

"So you're here to do a little reality testing?" Caldwell smiled gently.

"Yes."

"Welcome, Dani. I'm certain that we can help with your reality testing." Caldwell smiled and looked around the room knowingly.

Several participants giggled as though they shared some amusing secret. Dani was irritated at herself. Why did it matter to her what she thought of her agenda, she wondered. Dani didn't know what was bothering her. She was startled when she realized that Caldwell had finished greeting the participants and that she had not heard any of the introductions of the people sitting to her left.

Caldwell sat in front of the room in a plain chair. Her feet were flat on the floor and her arms draped comfortably on the arms of the chair. She looked the group over slowly.

"You are here, because the FAA has given you a priceless gift. Priceless." Caldwell paused for emphasis. "No amount of money could buy what you are given here today." Caldwell leaned forward, arms resting on her knees, hands folded together. "No amount. You are here from all over the FAA, for the single purpose of recreating." Caldwell stood and walked over to a flip chart and wrote the word out: "Re-Create-ing."

"This is what I mean by the word re-create-ing. To create means to bring something into existence out of nothing. When I create, I make something where before there had been nothing. To re-create means to create again. You have, each one of you, been given a second chance to be generative. A second chance to get it right. Recreating means the ongoing creation that you are beginning, starting today. The ongoing process of renewing yourselves, of rebuilding yourselves."

"So. Where do you begin this amazing processes of re-creating? Where do you begin? By acknowledging your nothingness. You are nothing. You know nothing. Unless you can empty yourselves, you will not have room for anything else."

Caldwell held up the glass of water that sat on the small coffee table by her chair. "Do you see this glass? If I tried to pour champagne into it right now, could I? Of course not. It is already full." She put the water down and stood in the middle of the room. "I am here to tell you today, that you are full. You are full of yourselves. Full of being right. Full of knowing. Some of you are even full of shit." She turned and smiled at the group. There were a few nervous giggles.

"You think it's funny." Caldwell looked at the offenders. "Well you're right. But the joke is on you. You are the joke. And you don't even know it. You haven't got a clue! Listen to me. Listen. Unless you can empty yourselves of all the crap, you will never have room to learn. So that is how you begin. You begin by emptying yourself."

Caldwell sat back down. "This is what we will do to help you. This is our commitment to you. First, we will provide you with healthful meals. Vegetarian.

This will help remove the artery clogging, mind anesthetizing sludge that has put you to sleep. Second, we will remove all caffeine. No coffee, no pop, no sweets. This will remove all the artificial stimulants you have become addicted to. Third, no one will receive or make phone calls from the outside. No one. Let go of your concerns about work. You're not indispensable. They'll get along just fine without you. Fourth, let go of your conventions about time. Time is not your concern here. Just because it's noon doesn't mean it's lunch time. Just because its 11 p.m. doesn't mean you need sleep. We'll decide when it's time to eat and time to sleep. You'll be amazed at how quickly your body will adapt, how little sleep you really need. And finally, there will be assigned bathroom breaks. No one will be excused except at assigned times. You will be amazed to discover how much control you have over your body."

"Are there any questions?" Caldwell looked around. "No questions. Very well then. You will find your room assignments downstairs in the main lobby. Load your things into your rooms, change into something loose fitting, like sweats. Be back here in exactly one hour with the pillows you were told to bring, and be ready for meditation."

Caldwell invited each participant to find a comfortable position, one they could maintain for some time, around the perimeters of the room and facing the blank white wall. They were free to use the pillows they had brought with them. Dani chose to sit in the lotus position with arms by her side, the back of her hands resting on her knees with thumbs and middle fingers forming a zero. Appropriate for getting in touch with nothingness, she thought somewhat sarcastically.

Caldwell told them to keep their eyes open and focus on a spot on the wall directly in front of them at eye level. She walked behind each of them slowly.

"Focus on the wall in front of you. From this moment on you are not to move or change your position. I will tell you when to stop." Several minutes of silence passed. Dani began to be aware of the urge to cough. She compromised and cleared her throat as quietly as possible. Caldwell was behind her. She felt her energy right behind her.

"Focus."

Dani went inside to a familiar place, born of years of solitude and quiet meditation, inside to the dojo she carried with her everywhere. Time passed. She heard a groan from someone in the room. It seemed very far away. Caldwell's voice was harsh.

"Focus. Don't move. You can do it. You are nothing. Your feelings are nothing. Send your spirit out in front of you. Empty yourselves." Throbbing, chant-like music filled the room. The music disturbed Dani and she frowned. It pulled her off center and took her into another world, unfamiliar to her, a world of pulsating rhythms and melodies that moaned. Time went by.

Across the room Dave's arms began to shake. His left foot had long ago fallen asleep and sharp pains were shooting down his back to the right leg. He tried to shift his weight slightly, but Caldwell was right there, urging him to focus. Dave was sweating with pain. The drops rolled down his forehead, into his eyes and down his cheeks. He felt dizzy.

"What kind of man are you?" asked Caldwell. "You can't sit quietly for a few minutes. Is this how a soldier behaves?"

Dave fought with all his strength to remain quiet, focused on his breathing. The crisis passed.

The music finished. Caldwell clicked off the machine quietly.

"Keep focusing ahead of you. You have done

very well. Now slowly begin to come back. You may change your position now. If you wish to lie down, you may. Take the time you need. Then meet in the dining room for our evening meal."

Dani slowly stretched out her legs and lay down on the floor to let her legs wake up. She looked at her watch and was surprised. An hour and twenty minutes had passed.

After a dinner consisting of lentil soup with chunks of tofu, plates of raw vegetables and loaves of whole grain bread, Dani had just enough time to splash cool water on her face to freshen up before the evening session. As she looked in the mirror, she felt somehow reassured to see her own familiar face looking back.

Back in the main room Caldwell told them to go up to each person in the room, stand, face them, look into their eyes and say "You are my teacher, I know you from of old." This activity was carried out quietly, broken occasionally by stifled sobs as some pairs hugged or experienced deeply felt emotions. Although the words at first felt strange to Dani, in a few cases, they felt congruent, especially as she went up to Dave. He was a manager in his fifties and had been a career military man before coming to the FAA. A certain weariness in his eyes conveyed that he had seen many things and had acquired a measure of wisdom.

It was about 10:30 when Dani glanced at her watch as they grouped together for their next activity. They were to pair up with someone in the room they did not know. Caldwell waited for them to find their partners.

"Now, place your chairs so you face your partners. Do it." Caldwell's voice grew firm as a few of them acted confused.

"You are to take turns. One of you will start. You will repeat this question, who are you, to your partner. Give them time to respond. Then repeat it again. You are to continue doing this until I tell you to stop. Under no circumstance are you to respond to questions or remarks your partner makes." She wrote the words Who are you? on the flip chart, then she nodded for them to begin.

Dani was paired up with Sharon, who no longer seemed cold. On the contrary, she was downright enthusiastic about the exercise and began energetically grilling Dani.

"Who are you?" Each time she asked, she tried a

slightly different emphasis. "Who are you?"

Dani, listening to others near her, noticed that at first the answers were somewhat formal and stiff. People began as she did, by saying their name or other descriptors.

"I am Dani O'Malley. I'm half Irish, half Italian." After five to ten minutes the answers became somewhat sarcastic.

" I am a person who is getting pretty tired of this exercise. I'm sick of this." After a half hour, some people were beginning to experience insights about themselves.

"I'm a person who drinks too much. I'm someone who is afraid to be close."

At about 11:15 Caldwell held up her hand and told them to switch. The questioner would now answer the same question.

At 11:50 they were told to stay with the same partner, but change the question. This time they would ask What do you want? Sharon dug in gamely. She looked into Dani's eyes and asked it over and over. Dani was getting tired. She had been up for 16 hours.

"I want to go to bed." She made various sarcastic comments, but since they didn't evoke laughter or change the subject, she began to think. What do I want. "I want to be able to trust. I want to believe in something greater than me. I want to have a family."

At 12:35 they were told to switch once again. Now Dani was the questioner.

By the time Caldwell gave the next assignment, the mood in the room was subdued. Fatigue was setting in. Several people were having difficulty staying awake. The question now was Why are you here? Even Sharon began somewhat grumpily.

"That's a good question," responded Dani, sarcastically. The exercise continued interminably. Suddenly, one of the participants, a nervous looking, short man from the FAA's legal department began to sob.

"I am here to find the truth." His partner posed the question yet again.

"I'm here because I have been blind." The man was crying now and others were starting to watch him. Tears and sweat flowed freely down his face, which glowed with insight.

"Now I see — I finally see." He leaned forward and grasped his partner's hand. The clean cut young man from ATC pulled back somewhat in discomfort. "Why are you here?" he tried to continue, embarrassed by the spectacle.

"I'm here because the universe brought me here.

I'm here in this moment, in this place so that I'd finally see." He got up slowly and walked over to where Caldwell sat in the front of the room. He knelt down and threw his arms around Caldwell's legs.

"Now I understand. I am nothing. I am empty. I am completely empty." He sobbed and then started to laugh wildly, joyfully. "I thought I'd find the Truth. But there is no truth. That is the truth. I am. Nothing more. Nothing less. I am." The man paused for a long moment. Then looking deep into Caldwell's liquid eyes he said solemnly, "You are my teacher. I know you from of old."

Caldwell gazed at the man lovingly and cupped her hands under his chin. It seemed that the infinity in her eyes streamed into his.

Chapter Ten: Engulfed

It was a grey day in the nation's capital as the spotless limousine slowly rounded the corner and passed a man walking alone down a side street in the Georgetown area. Someone inside the limo pushed the rear door open and the tall, slender man with sunlit hair and calculating eyes bent down to enter. Even after his eyes adjusted to the dark interior, he could not quite make out the face of the man occupying the back seat. A ceiling light, just above his own head, revealed the handsome, alert face of Andrew Maxwell.

"Good day, Mr. Maxwell," droned the voice in an impersonal way. Maxwell nodded acknowledgment. The voice continued. "I've been told that you are aware of the progress we're making in bringing about a totally independent FAA. We want more than anything to cut the crippling ties with Congress that have paralyzed us for the past 30 years."

The voice paused. The man in the rear seat searched Andrew Maxwell's eyes for his reaction.

"It's time to bring the FAA into the 21st century. The Senate is on our side. The antigovernment movement is gaining strength. The time is right. Our biggest obstacle is the House oversight committee. They've been sticking it to us for years. They use the budget talks as an excuse to shove their noses where they don't belong. And no one has a longer nose than Jim Martin."

"What do you want from me, sir?"

"Problems have solutions, Mr. Maxwell." The man reached into his coat pocket and handed a typed sheet of paper to Maxwell. "Here is a list of the flights Martin is scheduled to take in the next three weeks. We need to know how confident you are in your people."

Maxwell eyed the list quickly. "Absolutely confident, sir. Our network is now complete. Our people are in every part of the FAA — security, field maintenance, flight standards, aircraft certification, air traffic control. And," Maxwell paused, " even the NTSB. They are well trained. They'll solve the problem, sir. The investigation will determine a plausible cause and our initiatives will be invisible. "

The man leaned forward slightly and Maxwell caught a glimpse of his face as he spoke.

"Son, our mission is to create a 100% trained work

force, starting with the FAA and moving to the highest levels of the administration. People are crying out for leadership. Let's not disappoint them, son." The man with bad teeth leaned back into the shadows.

~

It must be about 3:30 in the morning, Dani thought to herself. She knew she was emotionally and physically exhausted, and judging from the others she was not alone. She noted that Maxwell had been absent for most of the day and returned sometime after dark, but no one seemed curious about his absence. He acted as though he had been with them all day and told the group he had devised a special experience for them. He and Caldwell blindfolded each participant and told them to sit quietly on the floor of the large meeting room. All chairs had been removed and the room was darkened, lit only by a few candles. Maxwell then clicked on the stereo and throbbing, sensuously primitive music filled the room. He told them to go deep within themselves, become one with the music and to express their recent experience with the group without uttering one word.

What then ensued was like some primal ritual with various people beginning tentatively to stand, moving toward each other touching faces, ears, throats. Small groups of two or three then slowly joined until everyone was connected. The mass of connected individuals began to take on an identity of its own and soon there were no individuals. This faceless anonymity began to bend and sway, expanding and contracting like a living thing, energized by an incestuous sense of danger and excitement. The music swelled, increased in tempo and pitch, then softened, slowed and was over.

Dani had no clear memories later as she lay her tired body down for a few hours of restless sleep, just vague impressions of throbbing sound and hands on faces, on arms, on hips. It was a highly sensual yet disturbingly alienating experience, knowing Maxwell was watching. Knowing that the omnipresent videocam was recording every move. As she reflected she felt a growing sense of humiliation. Why had she not walked out? She admitted that part of her was fascinated with the experience, part of her had wanted to stay.

Before closing her eyes, she realized that it had been days since she had sought the reassurance of her reflection in the mirror. She got up and in the dim light searched in her reflected image for something that would help her understand what was happening to her, but she found no answers.

Her sleep was fitful that night and she rose early with a headache. She went down to the kitchen looking for a cup of coffee. The cook, a slender, friendly young woman looked at her with concern. She peered around, making sure that they were alone and whispered.

"Why don't you take a cup of Caldwell's coffee. It has caffeine, and I think you could really use some."

Dani was startled. "You mean she doesn't drink from our coffee pot?"

"Oh no! None of the helpers and assistants do. We always keep the coffee separate. But please don't tell her that I let you."

It was the morning of the 13th day of Caldwell's executive training group. By tomorrow all would return to their families, and their high pressure jobs in the outside world. The two weeks were a blur to Dani. Like the others, she had lost track of time somewhere along the way. They never knew when they would eat or sleep. They rarely bedded down before 1:30 or 2:00 in the morning and then would rise at 6:30 for a 7:00 run on the beach. She had not known how difficult it was to run in soft sand. The hours of meditation, of countless exercises, of repetitive admonishing sermons by Caldwell blurred into a vague jumble of impressions.

That evening the group was once again gathered in the main room. All faces turned to the front of the room where Caldwell and Maxwell sat quietly. Dani's heart began to pound wildly. So far she alone had avoided being in the hot seat. Caldwell nodded imperceptibly at the man by her side, and he began.

"So. Dani. Did you get what you wanted from this session?" Maxwell's voice, while gentle, was unsettling.

"I believe I have," she replied tentatively.

"Do you recall what your words were?"

"Yes. I wanted to see what was real about your training."

"And you now believe that you do see what is real?"

"Yes."

"Would you say that you trust your eyes, Dani?"

"Yes, I do."

"Dani, please stand in front of the room and face everyone," Maxwell said calmly as he moved his own chair forward so he could keep his eyes on Dani's face.

She moved forward, wondering where Maxwell

was going, what he was up to. She felt flushed and had the distinct feeling that there was not enough oxygen in the room.

"You don't trust anyone," Maxwell stated. "You don't know the first thing about trust." He paused.

Dani didn't reply. She sensed that anything she said would only make things worse, like struggling in quicksand.

Maxwell turned to the group. "I want you all to close your eyes. Quiet your minds, and when you're ready, open your eyes and truly see Dani. Let one word come into your awareness that represents how she is being in this moment. Then share that with her."

One by one, they stood, looked into her eyes and shared.

"Fear."

"Alone."

"Cold."

"Proud."

"Afraid."

"Defiant."

"The group is telling you that they don't feel you trusting them, Dani. Each one has shared themselves with you." As he said this, he turned to the group and nodded.

Sharon spoke first. "I shared with you about

having an affair with my regional administrator. I risked my career. I trust you, Dani."

Then Dave spoke. "Dani," he said sincerely. "I shared about the years I neglected my wife and kids. How sorry I am about the past and how important they are to me now. I'm finally getting my priorities straight, and you were there for me. You listened. I do trust you."

Dani felt trapped. There was no where to run — no way out. She started to panic and could not catch her breath.

Maxwell motioned to Sharon and Dave to get on either side of her.

"Lay down on the floor, Dani." He said quietly but firmly.

Dani hesitated a moment, but then lay back as the room and the people faded. She drifted into the past

> I'm 4 1/2. I'm on a picnic with my
> parents. We're on our way home in the car.
> I'm almost asleep. Something happens to
> Daddy. He sounds like he's hurt. The car
> flies through the air and lands in water.
> Everything is dark. I'm in the back seat,
> and my seat belt hurts me. Mommy's
> making a strange sound, and Daddy
> doesn't say anything. I'm afraid. Water's

> coming in through the windows. I scream,
> "Daddy!" But he doesn't answer. I feel
> cold water on my feet. Water is filling the
> car. I untie my seat belt and shake
> Mommy's shoulder, but she doesn't wake
> up. I crawl over the seat between them.
> The water is up to my waist now. I step on
> Daddy's lap to get to the window. The
> water is too deep. Air rushes by me as I
> slip through the window. I see a light
> somewhere and swim toward it. There are
> weeds in the water and then I feel the soft
> bottom near the shore. I'm alone.

"What do you decide in that moment, Dani?" Maxwell's voice brought her back to the present. He was leaning over her, holding her hand.

"Decide about what?" She was bewildered.

"About who you can trust."

"Trust," she said. "There's no one to trust."

"No one?"

"Only me," she blurted out. "I can trust only me."

She sat up and Maxwell was looking at her. She was aware of no one else.

"You've got a lot to learn about trust — about surrender," he said softly.

Dani saw only of the blueness of his eyes.

Andrew Maxwell smiled at her, and she felt herself smile weakly back.

The morning of their departure had arrived and the group gathered for the final session. Caldwell let them wait quietly for a few minutes before she began to speak.

"Well done," she said lovingly to them, looking around the room at each person individually. "Well done. My name will be attached to each of you from now on, because you have re-created yourselves with integrity. We are now in a real sense a family, and you are accountable to one another. The time has come for you to leave, and you will be going out into an unconscious world. A world that does not understand integrity and accountability." She paused and looked at them gently.

"I don't want to send you into an unconscious and evil world without protection. I will give you each partners, friends who you can call when you feel weak. Friends who confront you when they see you lacking in integrity. I want you each to search your hearts. You already know who your partners are. Go ahead, stand and move toward each other and greet your new partners." Caldwell then watched as they stood one by one and began to form small groups of three or four. Dani did not move. Sharon and Dave came toward her and embraced her. Somehow she was not surprised.

Caldwell continued. "I strongly urge you not to speak about anything that went on during this session. Not to anyone, not to wives, partners, friends. People who were not here simply will not understand. Even though you love them, they don't have the context they need to understand. A war is going on in the world — a war over who sets the context. Over who decides what is real, what matters. Now, stay in your groups and each of you take turns role playing what to say when you get home and your significant other or best friend asks you what happened. Go ahead," she urged.

Sharon and Dave encouraged Dani to go first.

"Well, my closest friend is my neighbor, Bill." She smiled.

Dave smiled. "I'll be Bill. What's he like? What would he ask?

"Bill? Oh he's just an ordinary guy. He'll say something like, meet any new guys? Give me all the juicy details."

Sharon jumped in. "I'll play you first, and then you take your turn. It's easier when you see it with some perspective," she explained.

Dave got into character and said, "Hey — Dani, how was the workshop? Meet any new guys?"

Sharon responded ."Actually there were a few possibilities, but they didn't go anywhere."

Dave continued. "Well, I want all the details. What did you do each day. I mean two weeks is a long time. And why didn't you call even once?"

Sharon recited almost, it seemed, by heart. " They kept us very busy. Standard management training."

"But why didn't you call? I was worried about you."

"By the end of the day, I was so tired I just went straight to bed. I'm sorry I didn't call, because you're very important to me. Now tell me about you. What happened while I was away?"

They both turned with satisfaction and looked at Dani. It was her turn, and she went through the exercise just as Sharon had laid out. They knew this script forwards and backwards, she thought. She might as well stick to it. She looked at the two of them and wondered if anyone was conscious in that room. The question intrigued her. She looked around the room at everyone practicing exactly what they had been told. They all wore similar smiles and used nearly the same tone of voice in the role plays. She suddenly became aware of Maxwell watching her.

~

Early the next morning, Bill Lee picked up a cup of coffee and a copy of the Washington Post on his way to work. He stopped cold in his tracks as he read the headlines. "Plane Crashes in North Carolina Fog." He quickly scanned the article. "All 14 passengers and crew were killed instantly as the commuter plane plunged into a hillside late last night. Among the dead, Representative Jim Martin, long time critic of the FAA. Details are still sketchy, but the NTSB is on the scene and will provide further information as the investigation continues. What is known at present is that at the time of the crash, the plane was completely engulfed in flames."

Chapter Eleven: The Noose

Dani arrived home from the airport late in the evening. The flight home had been a blur. She had slept most of the way, tired to the very core of her being. As she climbed the stairs of the old apartment building which had been her only home for the past ten years, she was surprised to see Bill's door slightly ajar. He stuck his face out into the hall the moment he heard her footsteps and gestured silently for her to come into his apartment. She put down her suitcase and went to his apartment.

"Am I glad to see you." He closed the door behind her, hugged her and then stood back to study her face carefully over the rim of his glasses. The hug was out of character for Bill. He waited for her to say something.

"I'm glad to be back home," Dani said with a tired smile.

"Well, I want to know how it went. What was it

like.?"

"Oh, just your usual management training. Pretty exhausting." A shiver went down her spine as she heard herself use the words from her seminar practice session.

"The carpet cleaners came while you were gone. Your place smells great."

"What carpet cleaners?"

"Sit down." He led her to a kitchen chair and poured her some white wine.

Dani sipped it immediately and looked up curiously at Bill.

"While you were gone some men posing as carpet cleaners came to your apartment. You now have a very clean apartment and three state-of-the-art bugs. There's one in your phone, one near your answering machine and one by the sofa. They can hear you pass gas for Christ sake."

"Ex-nuns don't pass gas." She managed a grin. "Do you mean bugs as in hidden microphones?"

"Yeah. It's something I watch out for all the time because of my work, so Howie keeps his eyes open for me. He tipped me off and I brought a friend over to check the place out, a technical type. He claims they went through all your stuff. I suspect they were looking for the documents you left with me."

Dani had known Howie, their apartment manager for years, but she didn't know about the additional security services he provided Bill. She was beginning to think that she didn't know much about anything. It occurred to her that she actually knew very little about Bill and his career, and all of a sudden this bothered her. She had always felt secure with him, so why had she never pressed him to share details of his assignments.

Bill could see that she was troubled, but there were things that had to be discussed.

"Dani," he said tentatively. "I've been studying the documents you gave me. I'm convinced that's what they were looking for. Something is seriously wrong in the FAA. For one thing, Caldwell's training was purchased through noncompetitive bids. They chunked the training down to come in just under the legal limit. Somebody in the FAA wanted to make sure that Caldwell was the only one to get these particular training opportunities. And even more interesting to me, this preference for Caldwell and her training techniques is much broader than the FAA. I've been able to verify the claims that Caldwell or her henchmen have been training the IRS, the DOT and the Army's top brass. She's even been called in twice to the President's Council, but no one is willing to go on record about that."

"I ... I can't handle this tonight, Bill. I'm just too tired. I really need a good night's sleep."

"I understand."

"But what about the bugs. Are they still there?"

"Yeah. They are. Better leave them. You don't want to alert whoever put them there. Just remember not to say anything you don't want the world to know." Bill smiled reassuringly, but Dani had a distant look in her eyes.

Dani went back to her apartment, unlocked the door and carried her suitcase inside. As she leaned against the door, closing it behind her, the usual feeling of comfort, of security at being home was gone. In its place she felt a hollow numbness that slowly turned into a surge of rage. This was her space, her home. They had invaded her in more ways than one — and she felt violated. She wanted to scream but stifled it. Instead, tears came — silent testaments of her feeling of helplessness. She took a long, hot shower and slept a dreamless sleep.

It was Thursday. Somehow she had made it this far through the work week. Each day she felt a little more grounded. She had spent the first two days going through her mail and e-mail, just catching up. Then, the first call came. It was Dave, wanting to set up a weekly commitment group meeting. This was followed up the next day with a call from Sharon. Dani grimaced wryly, knowing they were working her like a tag team. She suspected that they wouldn't let up until a day was set, so she agreed to meet them for lunch each Thursday, starting today.

As she waited in the cafe near work she felt detached from herself, as though she was an observer, watching herself wait for two strangers she ordinarily wouldn't spend time with.

It was like old home week. They each greeted her warmly as they entered the cafe. How was she? How was she adjusting? What did it feel like — being back among the unconscious? Sharon shared that she needed their support so she would not weaken and agree to meet her married boss. A daily phone call would be appreciated. We have to hold each other accountable, she reminded them. Dave shared the happy results of his reunion with wife and family. She had been so understanding. Of course, she could not understand the profound experience he had shared with both of them, but he was trying to get her to take Caldwell's Couples Workshop with him. That way they could be true partners. He said he was grateful to have them to share this news.

Dani looked at them both, startled. They were waiting for her to share. In her heart, she was convinced that their intentions were honorable. They were simply being the best they could be. She wondered if they had any idea how they were being used.

"I'm happy to tell you both that I've come to an important decision."

They watched her eagerly.

"I'm going to take next week off and visit my foster parents. It's been so long since I've seen them. Besides, I think I need to reconnect with family." She smiled sweetly at them, not knowing where the idea had come from. It irritated her that she was at times the last to know when she had made a significant decision.

"Where do they live?" Sharon asked.

"Well they used to live in upstate New York, but they've retired to Santa Fe. It's been too long since I visited."

"Do you have their number so we can call and support you while you're gone?" Sharon said.

"Not offhand. But why don't we set up the time and place of our next Thursday meeting so we can get together when I get back?"

That afternoon she called the Robertson's from work. They were delighted that she'd be flying out. She arranged for round trip plane tickets to be picked up Saturday at the airport. Finally, she put in her request for annual leave. It was short notice, but nothing on her calendar would prevent it. Just as she was exhaling slowly with satisfaction, the phone rang. The voice belonged to Ana Estefan.

"Ms. O'Malley? Mr. Army would like to see you this afternoon at 4:00 if possible."

Dani looked at the clock on her wall. It was 3:50 p.m.

"I'll be there. No problem." His office was only three floors above hers.

Ana looked up from her computer and greeted her warmly. Dani sensed that this woman knew more than she let on.

"Go right in. He's expecting you."

"Dani!" Joseph Army's voice boomed. "Have a seat." He gestured to a chair. "I've just been on the phone with Dr. Caldwell and we were talking about you!" He emphasized the last word as though it was an honor to be mentioned in the same sentence as Caldwell. "She and I have concluded that you would be a solid addition to our Empowerment Team."

"I hadn't heard of that, sir. What's the Empowerment Team?"

"Well, you're aware that Caldwell is only one individual. She can only do so much. We've decided to form a select group of candidates for special, intensive training. They'll be trained in the skills that make Caldwell so effective."

"To what purpose?" Dani looked directly at Army.

"It's time to share Caldwell's ideas on accountability and integrity with the lower rungs of the FAA. So far it's been limited to high level execs like you and to upper and middle management. We've seen the benefits where her strategies have been embraced and it's time for the rank and file to be brought into the fold. There's too much victim-think out there. Too many dinosaurs terrified of change. The flakes who refuse to change need to be purged out of the system. All of us must commit 100% if we're going to bring this agency into the 21st century. What do you say?" Army eyed her carefully.

"Sounds like quite an honor. How many have

been chosen?"

"Well, the first year there'll be twelve. Caldwell wants to do it right. The next year those twelve will mentor another group, and so on. Let's see." He looked at a list on his desk. "I think you know Sharon."

"Pardon me, sir, but Sharon is not executive level. Why was she chosen?"

"You are new at this aren't you? Yes. You're right. Sharon's not yet executive level, but she's been chosen because of her at-stake-ness."

"Her at-stake-ness?"

"Yes, we put a lot of value on someone who lays everything on the line."

"When will this begin?"

"First Sunday next month. Can you set aside two weeks on your calendar?"

"Yes."

"Good. You'll get more information about what to bring and Ana will make all your travel arrangements. I hope you realize what an honor it is to be selected." Army looked at her closely. "I must confess, I was somewhat surprised when Caldwell demanded that you be part of this group." That was an understatement. He had been shocked that Caldwell would select someone so new to the agency and so untested.

Caldwell had hinted that the choice had been Maxwell's. He had insisted on Dani being part of the first group, against Elizabeth's better judgment. Army looked at the young woman standing before him. He had never really looked at her before. Long legs, full lips. What were Maxwell's intentions?

Army cleared his throat.

"By the way, have a nice time next week with your foster parents. Get plenty of rest." With that he dismissed her. He remained staring at the door after she left, remembering Caldwell's words. "She's very vulnerable right now. She's in the middle of working through several issues. Some basic decisions about life. Whoever is near her when she does, could have tremendous influence on the direction she takes, and I intend to be the one."

As Dani was leaving Army's office, she heard Ana speak to him on the intercom.

"I'll be right back. Just going down the hall." Ana caught up to Dani in the hall and cleared her throat. Dani looked at her quickly and realized she was nodding towards the ladies room. She followed Ana in. Ana first check the stalls to be sure no one else was in there, then she turned on the water and flushed a toilet.

"Don't drink the coffee," she said earnestly.

"Don't you mean the Kool Aid?" Dani retorted with sarcasm.

"I'm serious. They drug it. Not much, just enough to make you — more receptive."

At that moment another woman came into the room. Ana pretended to finish washing and drying her hands. She left without looking at Dani.

Chapter Twelve: The Initiation

The yacht anchored in Chesapeake Bay was only twenty minutes from the airport by launch and a short taxi ride. It was worlds away from those whose survival depended on their constant daily toil. The man on the bridge took a puff from his very long, very expensive cigar and slowly, deliciously held the taste in his mouth, feeling a gentle rush as the stimulants slowly found their way through the lining of his mouth and nose into his bloodstream. He exhaled and smiled. This was a good day at sea. He must, however, monitor his enjoyment. Self indulgence could be dangerous.

In the distance he could make out the ship's 17 foot launch returning with its solitary passenger safely concealed in the enclosed cockpit. He went below, stuck his head into the main lounge. "Our guest is arriving, gentlemen. It's time for us to take our places."

In the softly lit lounge, the admiral was quietly

conversing with Richard Burroughs, while Henry flitted around the room, his hyperkinetic energy not allowing him to sit still. Upon hearing Skippy's announcement, Richard and Henry excused themselves and went down the hall with him. Only the admiral remained to greet their guest.

Leading the way, Skippy unlocked the door to a small room adjacent to the main lounge. He turned on the lights and locked the door behind them. He then placed his finger in a small depression on the bottom of a book shelf. A fingerprint security device confirmed his identity and the built-in book case slid aside revealing a state-of-the-art recording studio. Skippy smiled at his companions, who shared his delight in technology as well as his passion for clandestine affairs. He flipped a switch, and four hidden cameras, strategically placed in the lounge, began to capture every word and gesture for display on the four monitors and recording on the digital tape decks before them.

Within a few minutes, a trim, white-trousered sailor announced the arrival of Andrew Maxwell. He then clicked his heels together and shut the door behind him without looking up.

"Andrew, you're looking fit as ever." The admiral nodded his head in greeting.

"Thank you, sir. A magnificent ship you have here." The young man's alert eyes assessed the quality workmanship and materials in the yacht.

"Yes. She's a perfect place for confidential meetings." He cleared his throat.

"Well, Andrew, the day has come to recognize your achievements and to reward your effectiveness. Welcome to The Second Ring." He smiled at the younger man and shook his hand.

"Let me list the reasons for this recognition. " The admiral gestured for Andrew to be seated. "You initiated and guided the FAA experiment. It was you who brought Caldwell in after the strike. You recommended her to various managers and executives until you solidified her position. You did this all invisibly." The admiral stopped for emphasis. "Invisibly. You used her to create a structure that pervades every part of the agency. And you have recently given us proof that you can control this structure efficiently and invisibly." The older man looked at him solemnly. "Our problem in the House oversight committee has been resolved, without extensive media coverage and without one word of suspicion. Truly elegant work, son."

Andrew Maxwell's handsome, slender face trembled with pleasure. This man's approval meant a great deal to him.

"I am today authorizing you to move strategically into all areas of transportation, land, sea and sky," the admiral continued.

"Do you recommend using Caldwell in these areas also?"

"It's up to you. You've rendered her expendable. Several others could now take her place. The decision is yours."

"I know Caldwell wants to reach down to the rank and file. I don't think we're ready for that just yet."

"I agree. The controllers in particular think they're America's last goddamn heroes, and their union has regained strength. If one of them so much as whines about a diversity training workshop, the union files a suit." The admiral lowered his voice. "Andrew, we must neutralize the union." He paused and poured himself some Scotch, then offered Maxwell a glass. They drank quietly for a moment.

Maxwell looked at the admiral intently as he continued.

"We don't want the fiasco that we had in '82. That was far too public. Gave them something to mount their resistance against.'

"Understood, sir."

The admiral slowly swallowed the last of the

Scotch. He leaned forward earnestly. "The unions are the deadliest threat that we face, Andrew. We can't allow them to set the context for the country. We can't let the lowest common denominator set the bar for the finest." He leaned back. "The members of The Second Ring are a highly select, handpicked group. They have proven themselves, as you have, to be masters of the strategic move. Able to influence without being obvious. They are masters of invisibility. Obvious power corrupts, but subtle power controls and endures unchallenged. Because of this, you will never know your colleagues, never be able to share their camaraderie. Your loneliness will be your greatest sacrifice." He looked sympathetically at Maxwell. "Do you recall The Principles, Andrew?"

Andrew cleared his throat. They had become his credo. He spoke in a calm, clear voice.

"Belief is the only Truth. Truth brings Transformation. Transformation brings The New Order. The New Order brings Justice. The Secret of the Ring is Belief. The Wearer is Invisible."

After Andrew Maxwell left, the four founding members of The Third Ring gathered in the main lounge.

"I've got to hand it to you, Henry. This ship is invaluable for our purposes. The tapes couldn't be more secure. The meetings more private. Impossible to bug. Never in the same place. No trace of comings and goings. A toast to you, Henry, dear friend." Skippy raised his drink slightly and smiled at his colleague.

Sir Richard lifted his glass. "And to you, sir, who brought to fruition the powerful idea -- An invisible force is an invincible force. Everything you envisioned is coming to pass."

The admiral spoke next. "To Richard, who has just landed our most promising candidate yet." He paused, because the news had not yet reached all ears.

"What do you mean?" Skippy asked.

The admiral smiled. "Who's the most invisible man in America?" He laughed when he saw the stunned delight in Skippy's eyes. They all tipped their glasses to Sir Richard.

"And last, but by no means least, to you, admiral, for being our visible connection with The Second Ring." Henry spoke with reverence. They all knew that the Admiral had volunteered for this task because he was less vulnerable than they to threats or blackmail. An advanced case of prostate cancer prepared him to sacrifice what remained of his life for their solemn cause.

~

Meanwhile, Bill Lee watched from the shadows as the launch docked in the small coastal town, saw the deputy director of training step onto the dock and disappear into a waiting car. The crisply dressed sailor who had piloted the launch tied it to the dock and hustled over to a nearby bar for a quick drink. After a brief delay Bill casually emerged from the shadows and followed the sailor into the bar.

The bar was dimly lit, almost empty. Two men were playing pool at the far end. No one sat at the tables. The sailor was sitting on a stool at the bar drinking a beer. The sailor and the bartender seemed to know one another. They exchanged a few lively comments and the sailor left without paying for his drink.

As the door shut behind the sailor, Bill, who had entered after him commented to the bartender. "Sure sails a beauty!"

"You got that right. She's no ordinary ship."

"It's the first I've seen of her."

"Oh, she comes by every month or so, when they

get folks from the airport. My cuz," he said, nodding towards the door, "says it's a cushy job. Hardly anyone there most' the time."

"Thanks for the beer." Bill thanked the bartender and left. His investigative instincts were screaming. He rented a small boat and moved out toward the yacht. A short while later, he anchored a discrete distance from it, took out a fishing pole and lowered a line over the side. After a few minutes he took out his powerful binoculars. Through the haze Bill Lee could just make out the name — Trilogy.

~

Back in D.C., the administrator of the FAA was having a fit. His secretary had just briefed him on a registered mail packet, sent by a former controller, claiming that the FAA was controlled by a guru and threatening to involve the media and Congress if it wasn't properly investigated.

"For God's sake, don't I have enough to handle? Congress has us drowning in paperwork, investigating crashes, investigating parts — their oversight committee should be called the over-and-over sight committee. I'm on TV more than I'm at home and I haven't had lunch. I don't have time for crazies."

"What should I do with it?"

"Let Army handle it."

Joseph Army got the request via the administrator's secretary. He immediately phoned Andrew Maxwell.

"I want you to handle the Morrow situation. He's threatening to go to Congress and the media. We can't have that."

Two days later an unscheduled inspection of Jake's plane took place after hours. The airport hangar that housed Jake's plane was coincidentally unattended that same night.

Chapter Thirteen: The AT-6

Dani spent two healing days in the Robertson's Santa Fe home. They talked and laughed and remembered old times. She loved sitting on the sofa between them, where it was safe and the world was a simpler place. They had done their best to see her through some rough times over the years, and she was grateful. On the third day, she got up early, went to a local electronics store and bought an answering machine. Back at their house, she helped her foster dad set it up. Dani wanted to protect them from any commitment group calls that might follow her. She also wanted to keep her whereabouts in the next few days secret. Later that morning they drove her to Albuquerque, where they dropped her off downtown and then went to visit relatives in a nearby suburb for a few days.

Dani went into a local car rental agency. She had hoped to pay for the car with cash. Recent events had convinced her it would be better if she didn't leave any trace of her movements, but they insisted on a credit card number. The ten hour trip gave her plenty of time to think about things. She tried to identify what disturbed her so much about what she was going through. It seemed clear to her that when a corporation or government agency violated the core values of an employee, they infringed on the most basic of all civil rights, the right to act according to ones own conscience. Even in the convent, where she had taken a vow of obedience, the teaching was clear. Her obligation to follow her conscience took precedence over her obedience to the laws of the church, at least in theory if not in practice. It was 10:00 that night when Dani arrived in Tucson.

The next morning as Jake Morrow returned to the hangar from a flight lesson, Tiffany, the flight school secretary teased him.

"Jake, I've got something for you." Somewhat miffed with his lack of interest, she lifted a long stem pink rose from beneath the counter and handed it to him. "All right" she complained, hands on her ample hips. "Who is she?"

Jake was startled. He didn't have a clue who it

could be from. He ripped open the attached envelope. The note said, Pima Air Museum - 2 p.m..

He inhaled the fragrance of the rose and chuckled at Tiffany's futile efforts to find out the identity of the mysterious girlfriend. Jake walked out of the office whistling. Privately he was wondering who had sent the flower and what it was all about.

~

He arrived at the Air Museum early. This had become his favorite refuge. On his loneliest days, he'd let his Harley lead him here, like an old friend who knew what he needed without wasting words. Once inside, his loneliness would fade. Maybe it was the desert, maybe it was the pain, but Jake had come to believe that the souls of the airmen who had once flown these beauties lingered nearby. Perhaps these planes were a link between heaven and the earth that their pilots were reluctant to leave behind. Maybe this was heaven — a huge celestial bar where tales of adventure and honor, death and despair were shared and understood.

He was distracted from his musings by the rear view of a woman wearing western style tan boots, cream cotton slacks tied with a tan leather belt, and a white cotton shirt. A straw cowboy hat hid her face from view. She was standing in front of a North American AT-6, the model that most of the aviators of WWII had trained on before they went on to their specialties.

"I remember pictures of my uncle in this plane," the woman said, sensing his presence. "I was told that he was killed on a bombing run during the war. His buddies nicknamed him the Red Bomber and I was named after him — his real name was Dan O'Malley.

As she turned, Jake felt a hint of embarrassment as he realized he had been admiring the backside of the chief internal investigator of his complaint. The sun, which was behind him, lit up her features. He was startled to realize how beautiful she was. She held out her hand in greeting and he took it. Unconsciously they let their hands linger.

"Thank you for meeting me here," she said, looking directly into his eyes.

"My pleasure," he replied with a smile. "This is my life." He nodded his head at the AT-6. "Actually, one just like it. I bought her eleven years ago and I've spent my spare time and money restoring her. It's one reason I became a controller — to be near planes, and to be able to afford my obsession." They were silent for a moment.

"The reason I'm here," she said, looking down at his hand still holding hers. He let go somewhat reluctantly. "The reason I'm here is that several things have happened since I spoke with you, and I have some more questions." They started to walk down the long row of planes resting on the tarmac. The Catalina Mountains rose from the desert floor off in the distance.

"What things?" he asked simply.

"Well, first, when I briefed the head of operations, I was told not to bother with a written report of the investigation."

"That figures." Jake shook his head. "They don't want anything in writing that could hold them accountable."

Dani nodded. "Second, I was sent to a two week training session and experienced Caldwell and Maxwell first hand."

"And how do you feel about your 'Caldwell experience'?"

"How I feel isn't as important as what I saw." She paused a moment, collecting her thoughts. "Not once either before, during or after, did I see any evidence of a medical or psychological history having been taken of any of the participants. Not once." Her voice was slightly higher than its normal calm tone. "Yet, profoundly personal issues were dealt with, and videotaped." Then she added, almost as a mental note, "Somehow I think if we could follow those tapes we'd understand what is going on."

"What do you think they do with them?"

She didn't respond, but the look in her eyes confirmed his suspicions. "You know what bothers me the most?" she said, looking at him. "You got fired because you objected to the training. On the other hand, in my group, mostly upper level execs — no one even questioned it. No one challenged them. Caldwell could have gotten us to do anything. Anything at all. And I include myself in that group. I knew what I was getting myself into, and it didn't help. They had me too."

"Do you think they don't complain because they like it?"

"Some, yes. I think some people feel they owe her a debt of gratitude, and they seem very genuine in their appreciation. But others are terrified. They're afraid to say anything negative, afraid for their jobs. Some even seemed afraid for their lives. I'm beginning to believe that Caldwell's a master hypnotist. She methodically puts these groups into a trance, then she tells them its the outside world that is unconscious, while they sit there and smile and nod."

"From what I gather, she used to be vicious in the beginning. I've heard the few who are willing to talk about it use language like "blood was spilled everywhere", or "she tore their heart out and stomped on it." The language they use is very violent. Now that she's well established in the agency and apparently in control, people come to the sessions advised to keep their mouths shut. The agency attributes so much power to her that she doesn't need to bully them into submission anymore. But bullying is at the heart of the dynamic." She lowered her voice. "I hate bullies."

Jake was startled by the anger in her voice. "I guess it's a case of survival of the fittest. It's a case of bully or be bullied. The bigger bully wins," he responded. "What concerns me is the effect all of this is having on the agency. It seems we are creating either bullies who control by threat and innuendo, or passive doormats who don't ever question or challenge authority. I don't want to see controllers forced into either mold.

"These men and women have to make split second decisions about peoples lives. On any given day, whether they're tired, or their wife has just left them, whether the kids at home have the flu, there's a thousand people in the air that depend on their ability to think for themselves. Maybe they are a bunch of smart asses who think they're god's gift to the world — but they also just might be the last American heroes."

They walked in silence for a few minutes. Dani looked up at him.

"I made some calls last week. Spoke to the cult education network. I think we're dealing with a full-blown cult. A government cult led by a government guru. Pretty scary, isn't it. Loyalty to the group above everything. She gives them her name. Diet is altered. No privacy. No rational dialogue. Pretty soon it's us versus them. Do you know she even sets up commitment groups to hold each other accountable between training sessions? Instead of SES, it feels more like the SS.'"

"You knew what was happening. You couldn't have been taken in?" Jake studied her face.

"Everyone can be taken in no matter how strong — maybe even because they're strong. I think the dynamic of a skilled hypnotist is a lot like an Aikido master. The key is to enlist the resistance. Take the strength of the enemy and use it to gain control. I know personally I have a weakness when it comes to hypnosis." She smiled self-consciously. "I had a friend who was a hypnotist when I was in grad school. I wanted to study hypnotism — so he invited me into a group he ran for overweight women. I was to be part of the group, watch his techniques and learn." She shook her head and smiled, remembering. "He said to me afterward that I was the first one to go under. We were all sitting on pillows around the room and apparently I fell asleep on the shoulder of the woman next to me with my mouth open and breathing in her face. He said he was laughing inside so much he could hardly continue." They came to the end of the row of aircraft and slowly turned back.

"You said you had questions?" Jake said.

"Yes. What's the status of your complaint?"

"Well, in the past nine months, I've sent packets documenting my complaint to the Southwest IG, the Southwest Regional Administrator, the director of training and finally last week, the administrator himself."

"How did they respond?"

"The regional people say the matter's not in their jurisdiction. The director of training said he'd have his deputy look into it. Do you realize who the deputy director of training is?"

They looked at each other. "Maxwell," they said in unison.

"Yes, Maxwell. I haven't heard from the administrator yet."

Dani nodded thoughtfully. "I don't know how to handle this investigation. Right now, you're the only person in the FAA I trust. Before I came here, I was told that Caldwell selected me to be part of a training team. She has hand picked me to become one of her disciples. On the one hand, it would be invaluable to learn more about what's going on. On the other hand — I'm afraid for my self. I know you were in special forces, and I suspect you have experience in dealing with brainwashing. Jake, I'm afraid these people will stop at nothing to achieve their goals. Can you help me?"

They spent the rest of the day engrossed in conversation. It was the first time Jake had ever canceled his flying lessons.

Chapter Fourteen: Air Born

Later that afternoon Dani told Jake that she wanted to visit the Saguaro National Monument before she headed back to Santa Fe. As a kid, she had been fascinated by the pictures in Arizona Highways that the Robertsons laid out on their polished cherry coffee table. When she had tried to picture her parents in heaven, it always wound up looking like an Arizona sunset. It never occurred to her that her instinct to protect her parents would keep them in a place where they would be far from water.

Jake persuaded her to leave the rental car at her hotel and go with him on the Harley. He mounted the bike and then turned to help her on. She swung her right leg over the seat as though she was born to ride. Jake began to suspect that Dani was a bit more complex than he originally had thought.

They followed the main road west, up through Gates Pass, down to the Sonora Desert Museum and continued into the desert. Except for the road itself, all traces of civilization gradually disappeared. As they leaned into the turns, Dani tightened her grip around Jake's waist. She was aware of every part of her that touched him and felt an ache that she had never known before.

They came to a valley surrounded by sloping hills. There were saguaros everywhere, all shapes and sizes. Jake brought the bike to a stop and they dismounted. They took their helmets off. The silence was profound.

"I know we're alone, but I feel like a thousand eyes are on us." Dani was almost whispering.

Jake nodded. "These saguaros are hundreds of years old. The Indians say that they are the ancient ones who watch over the land. They're protected here."

"I feel them watching us."

Jake smiled "When I first came to Tucson, there was a story in the paper. These two guys were out in the desert with shotguns using saguaros as their targets. They apparently had walked along shooting until finally one of the saguaros they had hit several times fell on one of them just as he was taking aim at another cactus. It crushed him to death. The Indians say he was punished for desecrating the ancient ones." He paused a moment. "Sadly, these ancient ones have more to fear from civilization than from a couple of nuts with guns. The city's spreading. Crowding them out. Pollutants are choking them. If we don't wake up soon, they'll be gone."

"I feel a comfort here," she said. "Maybe we're like them — lost in a world that doesn't seem to have a place for us. Sometimes I wonder if we'll survive."

"The desert is filled with lessons on survival, Dani. See how scrawny the saguaros are? We're at the end of a dry season. Monsoon's almost here. After the rain, they'll swell up, filled with water — and they'll hold onto it like misers, making it last through the dry times."

"What was that?" Dani exclaimed. She had seen something move, but couldn't make it out. It moved again. Then she saw a large rabbit with ears as long as its body. She instinctively took a step closer to Jake

Jake laughed. "That's a desert Jack. Speaking of survival, look at those ears. They're his way of cooling off, and his early warning system. Survival for the Jack is finding food, staying cool and avoiding predators like coyotes. Watch his ears." Jake motioned for her to hold still, then he snapped his fingers. The Jack held motionless but its ears instantly oriented to the sound. "He can hear a rattler half a mile away."

They both became more aware of sounds and Jake identified the scolding of a cactus wren, the soft wail of white winged doves and the evening call of quail. They watched as one quail family crossed the road. The female crossed first, followed by more than a dozen little shadows that scampered after her. The male stayed behind to protect the stragglers. Finally, after a call from his mate, he scooted after them.

Clouds toward the horizon began to turn all the vivid colors of an Arizona sunset. For the next ten minutes they were speechless. They and a thousand saguaros raised their eyes to the west in prayer. Nowhere on earth could the sunsets be more glorious. Nowhere could the passing of day be so revered.

The next morning, Dani drove her rental car to meet Jake at a nearby cafe for breakfast. They ate heartily and discussed plans. Jake would fly Dani back to Albuquerque where she'd meet the Robertsons. Then he'd return to Tucson and wait for a response from the administrator. She would attend Caldwell's next session and they'd play the rest by ear.

It was about 10:30 when they arrived at the hangar

where Jake stored the AT-6. He had decided not to file a flight plan. They would play it like she was a student and this was a lesson. The fewer people who knew who Dani was, the better.

Jake explained he needed to perform a preflight inspection. He looked into the cockpit to make sure all switches were off. Then he jumped down and began examining the left wing. His eyes carefully swept over the metal skin of the plane, looking for dents and other signs of hanger rash. Reaching the fuel tank located in the left wing, he opened the cap to visually check the fuel level and color. His fingers swept over the wingtips, again feeling for dents. He gently grabbed the left aileron and lifted it slowly, checking their mechanical soundness, looking for full range of motion.

Methodically, he moved alongside the fuselage, inspecting the radio antenna, examining nuts and bolts. As he reached the tail section, he checked the elevator for full range of movement. Finding no problems, he carefully flexed the rudder. Circling around the tail, he bent down to check the tail wheel, making sure it was in good condition, then he made his way back along the right side of the plane. As he reached the trailing edge of the right wing, he checked the wing flap and then completed a visual check of the fuel level and color of the right fuel tank. The landing gear felt firm as he kicked the tire. Everything passed his inspection. She was ready to fly.

Dani had flown all over the northeast on commercial airlines, but never in a small plane like this. While Jake completed some paperwork, she walked up to the vintage plane and rested her open palms on its seemingly delicate skin. What a history it must have, she thought. How many airmen had taken their first lessons on this very machine, and where did they go from there? Did they become bombardiers like her uncle? How many of them were still alive today? She had the oddest sensation that the plane had a story to tell, and a slight chill went down her back. She withdrew her hand quickly, unconsciously, and turned to Jake with the unanswered questions still on her face.

"Ready to take 'er up?" Jake asked. She hesitated imperceptibly but nodded eagerly. He gestured for her to get into the front seat and gave her an appreciative boost from behind as she stepped up onto the low wing and slid into the narrow cockpit. Then he was up on the wing, leaning over her and pointing out various controls: the rudder pedals, the aileron and elevator control stick, flap lever, throttle, prop control and mixture control levers. His enthusiasm was contagious. She began to feel how much he loved flying.

As they taxied to the runway she was moved by the audacity of it all. The raw nerve. To imagine they could get this metal body off the ground, to believe they could reach the clouds! As they rushed forward, Dani felt the plane come level with the ground as the tail wheel lifted off. As they continued to accelerate she began to tremble, not from fear but in anticipation. Suddenly the vibration and noise of the tires on the runway stopped and they were airborne. They climbed up, far above the valley floor and headed toward the Catalinas to the north. As they reached the first low lying clouds, Jake glimpsed Dani's face from the side as she peered down at the mountain range. Her joy was as transparent as a child's.

When they leveled off, he encouraged her to place her feet gently on the rudder pedals and follow his motions.

"Don't fight it. Just let your feet be led until you get the feel of it."

It didn't take Dani long to understand the relationship between the movement of the pedals and the direction of the plane. The stick controlled the ailerons and elevator and almost seemed to have a life of its own. She was somewhat disconcerted by its movement between her legs. The stick moved and caressed her inner thigh as Jake turned the AT-6 toward the northeast. She felt a mix of reassurance and excitement, realizing that it was Jake who was moving it.

"Whenever you feel ready, take the stick. Remember, I'm right behind you."

As she took control, the plane's nose rose slightly and she overcorrected.

"Easy, now. Remember, let the plane fly — don't make it fly."

She eased up on the control and let the plane have its way, her hand resting gently on the stick. Dani O'Malley was completely engaged in the experience of flight. Her soul was free and her heart pure.

Chapter Fifteen: Baptism

With occasional coaching from Jake, Dani had been flying the plane and enjoying every minute of it. Jake took the controls as they approached the Apache National Forest. He switched tanks, explaining to Dani what he was doing. He used the left wing tank for the first hour, then switched the fuel selector valve and flew on the right tank until it was empty. Subtracting one hour from the air time of the right tank gave him a solid estimate of how much time he had before needing to refuel. A few minutes after switching tanks, Jake noticed they were losing RPMs and the oil temperature was up slightly. He gave the plane more throttle. Dani noticed something different in the sound of the engine. She realized something wasn't right.

"What is it?" There was concern in her voice.

"We're heating up and losing RPMs." He opened the throttle, but it didn't help. The cylinder head temperature kept rising, the manifold pressure decreasing. Jake tried changing the fuel tanks by switching back to the left tank, but it didn't help. RPMs were still falling, and the oil temperature was getting dangerously high. Jake analyzed the situation. They were flying at 11,000 feet, about 2,000 feet above the local terrain. Visual Flight Rules applied. There were no standards, only exceptions, conditions and limits.

"I've got to shut her down," he stated calmly. "Take her in like a glider."

As she looked down, all Dani could see was a blur of mountain tops, rocks and pine trees. The situation didn't look promising.

"How can we land? It's all mountains down there." She tried to control her voice, to mask her fear.

"We'll find a way." Like any good pilot Jake was always observing, always calculating possible landing sites for just such an occasion. He already had his eye on the two lane road far below, winding back and forth between the trees. Given the glide path ratio he had to work with, it seemed best to bring her down as soon as possible. He shut the engine off rather than have it seize up. The plane became nose heavy and Jake eased back on the stick and retrimmed to maximize his glide path.

Without engine noise a deep silence filled the cockpit. For the next few minutes, he skillfully gave the plane its head. There was a fine art to gliding and Jake was an artist. For those few minutes they were one with the wind, but the silence was no comfort to Dani. She imagined that a plunge to earth ought to be accompanied by more noise and screams, but here they were, free falling and everything was so quiet. It was eerie. She didn't want to die like this. Passive. Silent. She wanted to scream with everything she had.

They were about a thousand feet above the pine trees that covered most of the area and he had less than a minute before he hit the ground. Every so often, a craggy rock formation jutted up from the forest. There were very few cars traveling on the road below.

"We'll go for that road," he said. "It's our best chance." Jake lowered the landing gear, but only one of the two green indicator lights came on. He tried again. The yellow, in-transit light indicated that the gear was on the way down, but one wheel was not completely locked.

"Damn! Landing gear won't lock." Now Jake's voice began to reveal his growing tension. Landing with one locked wheel could tear up the T-6 and increased the likelihood of serious injury to them. He decided to pull up the locked wheel and attempt a belly landing.

In front of them loomed the top of the highest

mountain in the area. They glided past the peak. There were fewer trees and more clearings on the far side of the mountain. Jake suddenly recognized the ski runs carved out of the pines and realized they were coming up on the ski lodge owned and operated by the local Apaches.

He spotted the small lake first, then the lodge. Across from it was a grassy field. It would have to do. He brought the plane in closer. The spring grass at this elevation was green and long. Hopefully, it would soften their landing and they'd sustain minimal damage.

Dani was having difficulty breathing. She stared at the control stick. Her instinct was to take charge, but logic told her that she had to trust Jake to bring them in. There was no other real choice. She clenched her fists and closed her eyes, while tears of helplessness and fear rolled down her cheeks. Then, suddenly she was thrown violently forward against the front panel of the plane.

> Jake was checking the plane, tracing his fingers over the wing tips, touching it the way he would touch a woman. But he seemed to know all along that the plane was her naked body and he smiled gently as he

caressed her bare legs, her hips, her arms, and undid her long hair. Suddenly, her novice mistress was standing over them frowning — scolding her for being late again for morning prayers. But Jake wasn't listening. He was watching the sunset. His wild hair was hanging freely, some strands sticking to his neck from the sweat of the desert heat. He turned slowly and looked into her soul for an eternity. The eyes were liquid pools. Suddenly it was Maxwell looking at her from across the room, flooding her mind. She had to get out, but she couldn't. The car was filling with water too fast. She couldn't breathe. Her lungs hurt so much. Daddy — help me. She struggled to get out the window but everything was so dark, so cold. She felt completely alone. Finally, in the distance there was a light. It was Jake standing with his back to the sun, calling her name. He came closer and with his strong arms, pulled her from the watery tomb.

Dani opened her eyes and saw Jake leaning over her, a look of concern on his face. She tried to focus her eyes. He smiled, the relief in his eyes evident. She reached up, put her arms around his neck. Her sobs, like those of a child, came freely for the first time since her parent's death so long ago.

Two local Apaches from the ski lodge helped Jake jack up the T-6 and force the landing gear down. They towed the plane to a nearby storage barn and then called the tribal chief, who was an old friend of Jake's and a fellow pilot. Jake shared his suspicions with the chief who was more than willing to let him hide the plane indefinitely on the reservation, where the authorities would never find it. The relationship between the tribe and the state authorities was distant at best. They spent the afternoon together, examining the damage and analyzing what had happened.

After a few hours of rest and some hot tea at the lodge, Dani joined Jake and the chief in the barn. The tension was gone from her face and she looked relaxed. A red bruise on her forehead was the only evidence of her recent trauma.

Jake straightened up and wiped his hands with a greasy rag.

"It was definitely sabotage," he said to Dani with

a frown.

"How do you know?"

"Someone put jet fuel in the right wing tank. We didn't switch to that tank for an hour, which is why we got as far as we did. There's a color difference in jet fuel, but for some reason I still don't understand, I couldn't tell looking in the tank."

"What would jet fuel do?"

"Jet fuel is basically high grade kerosene. It heats up the engine so it would seize up. We really had no choice but to turn it off."

"What about the landing gear, was that sabotage too?"

Jake nodded. "Somebody loosened the nut on the gear down line. That way I wouldn't notice the nut loose on the hydraulic line when I did the preflight inspection. I could pull the gear up when we took off, so everything seemed normal. But when I tried to lower the gear, it pumped the fluid overboard and then didn't build enough pressure to lock the wheel down. Whoever did this really knew what they were doing."

"Who would do this?"

"Someone who wants to keep us quiet. Very quiet."

Chapter Sixteen: The Stand

The chief was a big man who moved like a shadow and at the same time seemed rooted to the earth. He was a direct descendant of Cochise, chief of the Chiricahua Apache. He had flown Jake and Dani to Santa Fe in the tribe's private jet. After they dropped Dani off, the chief filed a flight plan that took them to a small airport just northeast of D.C. close to the Beltway. Jake had known the chief for eleven years, and although he called him his friend, he had never heard anyone use his nontribal name, George Walker, to address him. Somehow "Chief" said it best.

Jake told him about the entire FAA training affair and the chief offered Jake his help and any necessary resources without question. After flying in silence for several minutes, he turned to Jake.

"I will tell you a story, my friend."

Jake gave him his full attention.

"My people were desert dwellers as far back as

anyone can remember. They lived on the land beyond the Chiricahua mountains, in what is known today as southwest Arizona. It was there in 1861 that the white man's army arrested Cochise and his cousins. They accused them of stealing cattle and a white man's child. But these were lies. The white man wanted our land because of the river that always flows, that the brown robes called the San Pedro. They hung the cousins of Cochise, but Cochise escaped into the mountains. When the soldiers killed his father-in-law, Cochise became chief of the Apache. He and his warriors made a stand. They hid in the Dragoon mountains near Fort Huachuca and fought the white man for seven years. It was a fierce battle. The Stronghold of Cochise remains to this day. He was a great warrior."

The Chief paused.

"In 1872 Cochise surrendered to General George Crook. He trusted this white man who promised that his people would have their own territory where they could live in peace. But after Cochise died, two years later, my people were forced to leave their homeland. They were sent into the high country, into the cold and the snow, to a land the white man didn't want." The chief said sadly, "The desert is our home, Jake."

Neither man spoke for a long time.

"Jake, now you're taking a stand. You will never be able to go home again." The chief looked at his friend with compassion, then glanced over at a photograph he kept tucked into the control panel. It was a color photo of two laughing twin girls, his granddaughters. Jake had saved their lives. He would do anything he could to help him.

~

The study was simply but tastefully furnished. An elegant Persian rug lay serenely on the polished hardwood floor. The shelves along the walls were lined with books that reflected the broad interests of their owner: the subjects ranged from jurisprudence to sailing, from war game theory to the art of watercolors. There were novels from Dostoevsky to Ludlum. In the corner of the room stood a large well-polished desk, neatly stacked with folders and papers.

It was the end of a long day. Dusk had given way to darkness. The dim light in the study revealed a large, barrel-shaped armchair in the center of the room, facing the fireplace. In the winter flames would be crackling. Instead, a refreshing spring breeze filtered in through open windows on either side, blowing the curtains into gentle billows of gauze. The man in the chair, naked except for a pair of silk boxer shorts, removed his hearing aids, and slipped them onto the side table next to him. He put on a pair of well cushioned earphones and was instantly linked to the stereo across the room. The flick of a switch poured the passionate strains of The Moldau directly into his thirsty soul. He drank it in, feet grounded on the floor, arms resting on the arms of the chair. His graying head leaned back in abandon, his eyes closed. The breeze caressed his bare skin, urging him to relax, to let it all go. The world of Washington power and intrigue had for the moment faded. Healing waves of sound washed the dirt of the day from his weary soul.

Virgil Sinclair, the first African-American Investigator General of the Department of Transportation never heard Jake slip in through the open window and squat quietly on the floor in front of the fireplace. Jake waited patiently for the music to end. As the last strains of music ended both men were silent. Sinclair removed the headphones and opened his eyes. His life had been on the line for so many years and in so many situations, that fear was not his reaction. He looked calmly at the man, quietly sitting on the floor of his study, and immediately recognized that he could have easily harmed him if he had wished, while he sat with his eyes closed. He put his hearing aids back in.

"What are you doing here?"

"I need your help as IG, sir."

"Why didn't you call my office and make an appointment?"

"I'm supposed to be dead."

Sinclair studied Jake. "OK. You've got five minutes. Start by telling me who you are."

"My name is Jake Morrow. I'm a controller from Tucson. Correction. -- was a controller. I was fired for writing a letter of concern about management training in the FAA. For the past year I've gone through every chanel I know, regional IG's, regional administration. I've gone all the way to the top, to the administrator. But the only responses that I've gotten are 'it's not in my jurisdiction' or 'it's simply a difference in training philosophies.'"

"What do you think is wrong with this management training?" Sinclair's eyes narrowed.

"In my opinion, it's attacking the basic civil rights of individuals and creating an environment of fear. Individual's are afraid to disagree, afraid to question those in authority. I think safety is being compromised due to the training of Dr. Elizabeth Caldwell. She's been brainwashing the upper level of the FAA for almost 10 years. She has a say in who gets promoted, and who moves into the Senior Executive Service.

She's now branched into the DOT and has even trained some of your own investigators."

"My investigators?"

"Yes, sir. This training started at the top. Even your people are afraid to tell you what's going on. For all they know, you're in agreement with it."

"You make it sound like this Caldwell is in control of the FAA."

"It appears that she is. She tapes every session. She must have compromising information on almost every executive in the organization. Her influence is pervasive, and people are afraid to challenge it. No one knows how far it reaches."

"You said that you were supposed to be dead?"

"My plane was sabotaged. Very professional job. I was lucky to land her safely. I've hidden the plane and no one knows I've survived. I'd like to keep it that way for as long as I can."

"Why does this matter so much to you?"

"I love the FAA. I love it's mission. But something is wrong when people aren't allowed to think for themselves. Very wrong. I'm asking you to investigate it."

Virgil Sinclair frowned. He had been fighting the FAA for three years since his appointment. He didn't relish the thought of another battle, but thinking that some of his own investigators didn't feel free to come to him saddened him. "Do you have anything to substantiate your charges?"

Jake pointed to the desk where he had placed a large, manila envelope. "It's all there, a copy of everything I have. I also have a high level executive who's willing to talk — when the time is right. And, sir, you might want to examine Caldwell's videos. She's recorded intimate information on almost every high ranking agency official."

Sinclair walked over to his desk and picked up the envelope. "How do you know you can trust me? How can you be sure I'm not one of them?" he said, turning.

But Jake was gone and the curtains billowing gently at the open windows whispered his reply.

~

Bill Lee arrived in his D.C. apartment late that night. He had been on the road for nearly two weeks. Several years back, he had set up a message relay service to ensure confidentiality and safety for his sources. He had long ago given the number to Dani, a secure way she could call him if she ever needed him while he was on assignment. After dialing one number, a correct password sent the caller on to another location. There were three loops in all, with three sets of codes that were regularly changed for security. As he listened to his messages his heart started pounding when he heard Dani's voice.

"Bill?" She sounded worried. "I went to Tucson to meet with Jake Morrow. We're both committed to uncovering what's going on in the FAA. Someone sabotaged the plane we were in and it crashed, but we're both OK. I'm heading back for two more weeks of training in Alexandria. Jake is in D.C. You can reach him at the Regis. Bill, I want you to use the materials I gave you in whatever way you think best."

After the message ended, Bill turned off the machine. He wished Dani hadn't gone to the next training session. She was in over her head. This thing was bigger than any of them had imagined, and she didn't have a clue about the kind of people she was dealing with. He should have been more open with her. Should have warned her that these men would stop at nothing to achieve their goals.

~

When Jake didn't arrive back at the hangar within a few hours, his coworkers assumed he intended to stay somewhere overnight. A mechanic in the hangar had seen him take off for a lesson with a female student. The mechanic said she was a looker and the secretary jealously recalled how she had sent Jake a rose. But after two days of canceled lessons, their concern grew and they filed a missing plane report. No one had seen or heard from Jake Morrow. They began calling various airports where he might have headed, but there was no hint as to his whereabouts. They each hoped that Jake had at last fallen in love and that that explained his unusual absence, but as each day went on the likelihood of a happy ending decreased.

In Phoenix, the news that Jake's plane was missing reached the desk of Bob Jacobs, who was visibly shaken. The visiting head of security happened to overhear the news. Later that day he called Washington from his hotel room.

Maxwell picked up the phone on the first ring.

"It looks like Morrow's plane went down. They haven't found the wreckage yet, but that could take time given the harsh terrain around Tucson. Supposedly he was with a woman. No. No ID on the woman. Local girl, I think. Taking a lesson."

Maxwell snarled, "You know better than to assume anything. Get the facts. I want to know that every aspect of this problem is solved. I want to be sure there are no complications. Call me when you've got all the facts." Maxwell hung up the phone. He would inform Army that the Morrow matter had been resolved.

Chapter Seventeen: The Investigator General

Jake's mysterious appearance and sudden departure left Sinclair with mixed feelings. He sat down and stared at the manila envelope. The sense of well-being induced by the powerful strains of music was gone. In its place, resentment about the invasion of his personal space competed with curiosity about what the envelope contained. Sinclair waited, as if watching some imaginary scale slowly, inevitably shift out of balance. Curiosity winning out, he finally emptied the manila envelope onto the desk and studied the contents thoroughly. He read through Harry's analysis of the contracting irregularities, copies of Jake's complaints to various agency authorities and lastly the packet of Dani's conversations with managers, their names and positions redacted to protect their identities.

The situation seemed straightforward enough.

Certain individuals felt abused and outraged by Caldwell's training. That by itself was almost to be expected of any program with teeth in it. What was unusual were the contracting irregularities and suspicious incidents that hinted at a cover up. The contracting violations sounded a warning note in Sinclair's mind — an I.G. must be ever vigilant about the potential misuse of taxpayer monies. This alone warranted further investigation. The coincidence of Harry's fatal heart attack at a training seminar and Jake's near fatal plane crash after his formal complaint was too much to ignore. And yet, what bothered Sinclair was a nagging sense of the widespread influence of this training. He was disturbed by the measured response from those interviewed, reflecting an almost identical wording. And finally there were Jake's words about Sinclair's own people. Members of his staff had taken the training and he didn't even know about it. He needed to verify these allegations and do it quickly.

The next morning, he called in his office director and shut the door. Barbara Buffalini had been in her position longer and knew more about the daily operations of the department than he ever would. He had relied on her to keep things running smoothly while he tried to light fires under Congress and the

FAA. She had been nominated by his predecessor to the department's Executive Development Program, which prepared likely senior executives for their future responsibilities.

He watched Barbara come into the room. She walked with a large ungainly stride which when coupled with her name, had resulted in the unfortunate nickname Buffalo Babs. On one occasion when she was on travel, he had overheard some of the staff singing a hearty rendition of Buffalo Girls with comedic flair. He gathered that there was little love lost between Barbara and her staff. He himself never had a problem with her. She had an ingratiating, almost flirtatious quality in her dealings with him that he disliked, but it did not interfere with her job performance.

"Barbara, thanks for coming. Sit down, please."

She looked at him quickly, sensing something out of the ordinary.

"Barbara, what can you tell me about Elizabeth Caldwell?"

"Dr. Caldwell?" Her eyes lit up. "She's the best thing that ever happened to this agency. Did you have anything specific in mind?" She seemed eager to continue.

"Yes. Has she ever trained any of our staff?"

"Yes, sir. Just before your appointment. We were experiencing some staff, um...problems at that time, and she came in for a three-day intervention. Things have been running smoothly ever since."

"What kind of staff problems?"

"Oh, you know. Grumbling, backbiting. Disgruntled employees. There was a real lack of team spirit, but that's all changed now."

"Who recommended Caldwell, if you can remember?"

"Yes, I can. It was the deputy director of training, Andrew Maxwell," she said proudly.

Sinclair nodded. "Thank you, Barbara. By the way, I'd like you to arrange brief individual interviews with me and your entire staff for this afternoon. It's something I should have done a long time ago. It's about time I got to know them better."

She looked up at him, quickly covering up the suspicion in her eyes, but Sinclair was an astute observer and caught the glance.

"Is there anything wrong, Barbara?"

"Not at all. I'll get everything lined up for you." She smiled sweetly.

Sinclair stifled a yawn and looked up at the clock. It was almost 4:00, and he had spent the last several hours in interviews with his staff, going nowhere steadily. It was apparent to him that they didn't trust him and were suspicious of his motivations for meeting with them. There was only one more person to meet and it was getting close to carpool time. Maybe he should put the last interview off until morning. He sighed. On a scale of one to ten, he deserved a big zero as a manager, he thought critically. You don't wait for a crisis to get to know your people. His years on the bench had taught him that much. But Washington bureaucracy had a way of paralyzing the best of intentions.

There was a knock at the door. He looked up to see Carla Sweeney, his last appointment.

"Come in, Carla. Have a seat."

"Thanks." She waited for him to initiate the conversation.

"Carla, let me start by apologizing for not taking more time to get to know you. I'll be straight with you, however. I do have an agenda for this meeting." He paused.

"How can I help you?" she said.

"You can tell me about the training you attended with Dr. Caldwell." Sinclair watched as she lowered her eyes.

"It was OK." Her response was unenthusiastic. "Why are you interested?" She looked directly at him.

"To be honest, I've heard some complaints recently and wanted to get more information. I just found out that about half of the people in this office had exposure to Caldwell a few years ago. I was hoping that you might help me."

"What have you heard?"

"Some people felt she was incredible, others... abusive." He looked up, startled, as Carla laughed out loud.

"Well you heard right. Look." She leaned forward. "I've got nothing more to lose. I'll be retiring in less than a month." She paused and looked at him thoughtfully. "Caldwell's training was the most divisive thing that ever happened to this office. You look surprised, but within two months of that training, more than half the staff transferred out. I stayed because I only had a few years to go, but the younger ones got out while they could."

"What was so bad?"

"I'll give you an example. There was one typist who smoked. Caldwell attacked her relentlessly and told her she had no self control. That she was poisoning not only our air, but our team. She convinced the woman that she was a worthless piece of garbage." Carla's voice trembled with anger. "She'd give these interminable lectures about taking responsibility. About accountability and integrity, but..." Her voice trailed off.

"But what?" Sinclair prodded gently.

"But what I saw her do had nothing to do with integrity. She would criticize and ridicule us until we had no self esteem left. It was almost like a calculated attack."

"What was she attacking?"

"I think... and believe me, I've thought a lot about this. I think she was brought in by Barbara to get rid of people she thought were troublemakers, and to break the rest of us so that there would be no doubt in anyone's mind that she was the boss. I'd swear that Barbara gave her a hit list and that Caldwell worked the list."

"If half of you left, she must have been effective."

"You'd better believe it. She was ruthless at eliminating problems. She'd also pry into really personal things. Things I didn't think she had any business going into."

"How personal?"

"Well, like religion... or sex. She picked on one Catholic woman because of her views on birth control.

She kept getting pregnant, you know. Caldwell ridiculed her for that. She'd pry into how many marriages someone had been through. But all of it seemed to be aimed at breaking our spirit. She treated us like children, as though Barbara was our parent. She even said that Barbara had given us her name and knew what was best for us, whatever that meant."

"Did anyone fight back or argue?"

"You've got to be kidding." She looked at him with a sad little smile. "It was clear to everyone after a few lengthy, brutal attacks that it was in our best interest to keep our mouths shut. It was just too expensive to try to argue."

He looked at her. "You don't seem the kind of person to lay down without a fight. What happened to you?"

"Me? Boy — it's been a long time. I've never talked about it to anyone."

Sinclair waited.

"You're right. I wasn't my usual feisty self. I had just had a mastectomy and I was taking radiation treatments and feeling pretty lousy." Carla cleared her throat and nodded as though giving herself permission to say it out loud. "She told me that I was the cancer that was destroying the office." Carla looked down at the floor. She didn't cry. She didn't do anything. She just paused and with a cold resolve continued. "Can you imagine somebody that cruel? I'm much stronger now. I'd love to run into her now. There's a part of me that would give anything to destroy her, the way she destroyed so many of us."

"Did she have anything to do with other parts of the department?"

"Yes. Isn't it bizarre? Here you have a nut like her training our agents, so that if anyone investigates her, they have to report to one of her followers. Clever, isn't it? She's trained almost every part of management in the DOT."

Sinclair looked at her puzzled. "I thought this was confined to the FAA."

"No way. She's trained every section of DOT management. I tell you, she's everywhere. To tell the truth I thought you were no different than the others — that you knew and approved." Carla looked at him. It was clear from the look of disbelief on his face, that he did not.

"Now we have managers who follow her model," she continued. "They use control and confrontation to manipulate their staff. Confrontation is the big word now. If you have a different point of view they confront you for not being a team player. No, Mr. Sinclair. This thing has spread all through the department. I'm dating a manager in the NTSB and he has even more bizarre tales. They had one session where they sat around in their underwear and had to reveal their sexual fantasies. It's really sick. Of course, Caldwell didn't lead that one. That was Andrew Maxwell. I hear he's quite good at stripping people of more than their clothes. He goes for the jugular."

"Their underwear?" Sinclair was incredulous. "Are you sure this was management training?"

"Executive level." Carla nodded.

"Would your friend be willing to talk to me?"

"I really don't know. Everyone's so afraid that if they talk they'll lose their job or —worse. I don't know if he'll talk to you. But I'll ask him tonight."

Sinclair stood and reached for her hand with both of his. "Thank you, Carla. Thank you very much for being open with me. I'm sorry for what you went through."

Later that night, Carla phoned Sinclair at the home number he had given her.

"He'll talk to you, Mr. Sinclair, but first he wants a promise of confidentiality."

"He's got it. This information is for me alone."

There was a silence at the other end as Carla hung up. The lack of dial tone told Sinclair that her friend had been on an extension and was still there.

"This is Virgil Sinclair. Carla said that you've had experience with Maxwell at the NTSB. Is that true?"

"Yes."

"How would you describe the training?"

"Abusive. Abusive and sick."

"Why did you attend? Why not leave?"

"Nobody leaves if they value their job."

"What do you see as the purpose of the self revelations?"

"He used what we said to humiliate and ridicule us. I don't know how to say this, Mr. Sinclair, but Andrew Maxwell, um... well he gets off on bending you over and... to put it politely, sir. He likes to screw with peoples minds and hearts."

Sinclair was quiet.

"And to think that this was paid for with taxpayer money, sir."

The I.G. shook his head silently and agreed.

"And promoted and protected by the agency and the department."

Virgil Sinclair suddenly felt very old. He tried to analyze the situation. What was the point of the training? He suspected that it wasn't abusive for it's own sake. No, sick as that would be, this was more insidious. This was about taking control. But of what? He had thought it was limited to the agency, but now he wondered if there were any limits. Was the agency already out of control? How far did it go? Who was behind it?

Chapter Eighteen: Warriors

To the front desk clerk at the Regis, Jake Morrow was just another in a steady stream of Apache's who occupied the tribal suite while visiting the nation's capital. Some came to visit the monuments. Some, to lobby congressmen and senators. In Jake's case, the clerk guessed the latter. Steel blue eyes betrayed a mixed ancestry, while the man's bearing and intensity indicated that he was in every sense a warrior. Just registering for the tribal suite was all the disguise Jake needed.

The clerk rang Jake's room to announce that a Mr. Lee was waiting for him in the first floor bar. As Jake took the elevator down to meet him, he couldn't help wondering about this man who had been Dani's longtime friend. He paused inside the door of the dimly lit bar until his eyes adjusted. Scanning the room, he made eye contact with an oriental man who stood and welcomed him with outstretched hand. His elegant bearing conveyed both openness and mystery. Jake returned the greeting warmly. He wondered what Lee's story was. Sometime, when this was all over, they'd talk over a good meal, but today they had to stay on task.

Lee spoke first. "I've studied the file Dani gave me and the material you shared with her. It's helped me fill in some missing pieces."

"Do you agree with our assessment of the situation?"

"Yes, as far as it goes. But I have solid evidence that this is much bigger than the FAA."

"We realize that Caldwell's influence is broader. She's worked with the IRS, DOT, and even some Army brass."

"No, that's still not big enough, Jake."

"What do you mean?"

"Caldwell's only the tip of the iceberg. There's a very secret, very powerful group pulling her strings — with intentions to control much more."

"Is she part of this group?"

"I don't think so. I don't think she even suspects what's really going on. She's under the illusion that she's calling the shots." For the next hour, the Post's investigative reporter briefed Jake. He shared the facts he had uncovered over the past few months, and his hunch that the problems with bogus parts, uneven inspection, aging aircraft and the abusive training were all somehow related. He had come to the conclusion that the key to understanding the big picture rested with Andrew Maxwell. And Maxwell had led him to the Trilogy. Finally, Bill leaned back.

"Well, that's where it stands."

Jake looked down at his hands for a moment and swallowed. "Changing the subject, Bill, I'm worried about Dani. I don't like this situation she's gotten herself into. These people are dangerous. They will destroy anyone who gets in their way." Jake smiled slightly, but more than just friendly concern showed on his face. He may have been unaware of it, but he was beginning to look like a man in love.

"Don't sell Dani short. She's tougher than she appears." Bill's voice softened. "Don't worry. She'll find her way back." Bill's eyes moistened as he studied Jake's face.

Jake nodded, slowly aware of Lee's compassionate gaze. "What's our next step?"

Lee laid out the plan. He wanted to get on board the Trilogy. It was the best lead he had. The only hitch was financing. He was limited by a reporter's expense account.

Jake smiled. "I don't think money is our problem."

He brought Lee up to speed on the chief, and the new gaming laws that had created an abundant source of cash for the tribe. Bill's reaction was nearly imperceptible, a single, happy blink. He immediately began making lists of equipment they would need and actions to be taken.

~

Joseph Army didn't appreciate the 3:00 appointment Virgil Sinclair insisted on scheduling for Friday afternoon. It was unspoken etiquette in D.C. not to interfere with an executive's weekend plans, which generally began with drinks around noon. Unless something urgent demanded attention.

Sinclair swept into Army's office without giving Ana time to announce his arrival. He had learned to shield himself from the head of operation's brusque receptions by being brusque himself.

"Well, Inspector. What brings you here today?" Army emphasized the word "today" with a beleaguered tone in his voice.

"You can be sure it isn't good news, Joe." Virgil took out an inch-thick, bound request for investigation of Caldwell's executive training program from his briefcase and handed it to Army. "I've got to follow through with this. There are too many unanswered questions that need to be resolved. Too many documented infractions that must be investigated."

Army threw the report on his desk. "You don't know what you're doing, Virgil. You don't understand the harm you will cause. Do you know how long it's taken us to get this program in place? The money we've invested in it? Do you know how many people have benefited from it? For every person who complains, there's a hundred who'll swear that it's effective. For god's sake, you're listening to disgruntled employees."

Virgil shook his head. "The evidence is compelling, Joe. I also want Caldwell out, at least until the investigation is completed. No training, no contact. Is that clear?"

Army was shaking with rage. "You're ruining more than you can possibly know. Call this off while you still can, Virgil."

Virgil Sinclair stood and looked long and hard at Army.

"I'm just doing the job I was hired to do, Joe. To investigate, and make sure the good of the flying public is being served — that's my duty. If nothing turns up, you can go back to business as usual. Surely you have nothing to fear from an objective investigation?" With that the IG walked out.

Army closed the door, unnerved. He hadn't seen this coming, never thought it would get to this point. He went over to his desk and poured himself a shot of the whiskey that he kept in his bottom drawer for just such an occasion. Calmer, he got on the phone and began to dial Elizabeth Caldwell, but thought better of it. When it came right down to it, it was every man for himself. He'd hang her out to dry in a minute, to save his own skin.

~

The call came as Elizabeth Caldwell was about to begin the opening session of the new Empowerment Team's training program. It was Andrew Maxwell. As she listened, her legs buckled slightly under her. She leaned on a table in the hall of the Alexandria mansion they had rented for the next two weeks. She steadied herself, then lowered her body slowly to the chair. She would get on top of this. She just needed a minute.

"Are there any tapes or files outside your office?" Maxwell said.

"No. No. Everything is there. You've got to get there before the I.G. does and get them for me."

"I'll take care of them." He lowered his voice.

"Elizabeth, don't say anything or admit anything. Do you understand?"

"What's going on, Andrew?" Her eyes were searching the room, the walls, the ceiling as if looking for answers. Then her voice grew stronger. "The bastards! I'll get through this, because if I go down, thanks to those tapes, half the management of the FAA will go down with me." Just then, Caldwell heard the front doorbell of the mansion ring. It would be the agents from the IG's office. She distractedly hung up the phone and walked slowly down the long, dark hall to the door. She wondered what the south of France was like this time of year.

Andrew listened to her with contempt. She really had no clue about what was going on. She had assumed that she was calling the shots. All those years, while she thought she was curing him, he had been observing her — learning, studying every move, until finally one day he had surpassed her. It was inevitable, really. The student must surpass the teacher. Besides, her world view was just too limiting. Within the context she had set, she was completely in control, but she wasn't ready to up the ante. She wasn't ready to play with the big boys. Andrew, like Caldwell, had little compassion. Neither of them was limited by what they considered antiquated codes of ethics. They were in the truest sense sharks and found life to be quite simple. In any given situation, the person with power was the one with more options. Maxwell had simply cultivated options that Caldwell hadn't considered. He would stop at nothing to achieve his goals. He was ready. It was time for him to come into his own.

In Caldwell's Beltway office, Maxwell hung up the phone. He had taken tapes and folders out of the drawers and file cabinets and methodically strewn them around on the floor. He poured kerosene evenly around the room, guaranteeing that everything would burn to ash. As he lit the match and watched the flame race around the room, a dark smile curled his lip. Ordinarily, Andrew Maxwell would never get so directly involved in a clean up such as this, but he trusted no one to completely eliminate the damning notes that Elizabeth had taken about his own visits in earlier years. On a primitive level, he screwed his therapist one last time.

He closed the door as his past went up in flames, along with hundreds of executive training tapes. He was across the street when the first fire truck rounded the corner seven minutes later. An incendiary device he had placed in the office below hers went off, creating even more commotion. No one noticed the well dressed young man slip into the front seat of a grey BMW and drive away.

Chapter Nineteen: Burnt Offering

The twelve Empowerment Team members had spent the few hours since their arrival exploring the Alexandria mansion, finding their assigned rooms and debating the fate of the recently dismissed Dr. Caldwell, whom the IG's agents had so rudely confronted. They were called to the main gathering room and had just assembled as Andrew Maxwell entered the room. He looked around at the participants, mentally noting each one and recalling their history. He had influenced Caldwell's choice and was pleased with all but one. Tom Filipiac, a slightly overweight man in his forties, associate director of the Office of Safety Standards. He had argued against Filipiac's participation in the program, but Elizabeth had prevailed on this one.

"As you all know, Dr. Caldwell has been removed," He stated. "I am taking her place."

The tension in the room rose dramatically.

"Over the past eight years we have trained several

thousand of the brightest and the best in the FAA. It is now time to broaden the influence of our leadership. It is now time to extend our influence throughout the agency and beyond." Maxwell looked around the room. He spoke slowly, deliberately. "Let there be no doubt in anyone's mind. You have freely chosen to be here. From this moment on, each of you is competing to remain in this program. If you don't like it — get out now. There are many waiting to take your place. Does everyone here understand my meaning?" Heads nodded in affirmation as all looked to Maxwell. Each strove for a subtle invisibility hoping to avoid becoming the object of their new leader's scrutiny.

He looked around the room. They were all sitting in comfortable over stuffed sofas and chairs. They are so soft, so undisciplined, he thought with contempt. They needed to be challenged. He would confront and purify them. He would regenerate them until they became perfect tools, instruments for him to fashion the ideal society. His unspoken wish to clone himself was about to be actualized.

"It is time to bump up our level of commitment. Stand up." Everyone stood up immediately, although it wasn't easy getting out of the soft furniture.

"Sit down." Everyone sat. Two women glanced at each other, assuming that was the end of the exercise.

"Stand up."

"Sit down." The commands seemed endless. He continued for forty minutes. Then he looked around the room.

"Dani, come up here. Sit next to me and observe."

Dani went to the front of the room, where Maxwell gestured for her to sit in a small chair next to his. He then continued with the exercise for the next ten minutes.

"It's a different perspective, isn't it?" He said to her so everyone could hear.

She nodded in response.

"Become aware of what you observe," He continued. "Stand up. Sit down. Who would you call on, based on your observations?" He asked her.

Dani had noticed Tom appear to grow more resentful as the exercise continued. He was emitting audible sounds of displeasure, rolling his eyes and lagging behind the group in getting to his feet.

"I'd call on Tom," She said.

"And what would you ask him?" Maxwell was pleased with her choice.

"I'd ask him if he wants to be here?"

"Go ahead — ask him." Maxwell's voice was supportive.

"Tom, do you want to be here?"

"Of course I do." Tom responded gruffly.

"Your words say yes, but your voice and face say no. Which is it?" She asked. There was no tentativeness in Dani's voice. Maxwell suppressed an impulse to look at her and kept his focus on Tom.

"This is stupid. It's supposed to be an advanced leadership course, instead he's treating us like children."

"And you object to being treated like a child?" Dani asked.

"Of course I do. I'm the goddamn associate director of safety standards. I've got more important things to do than play some parlor game." He was defiant.

"If you're unable to see the value in this exercise, I suggest you attend to those more important things." Dani turned to the rest of the group. "Does anyone here think it's childish to follow orders?" There was silence. "You're here to learn about yourselves. In a given moment, anyone presented with a strong stimulus, like the command to stand or sit — has an immediate, unguarded reaction. That reaction will tell you more about your true attitude than the mask you usually wear. That moment presents you with an opportunity to learn about yourself. About who you really are."

A film of fear appeared in Tom's eyes. He was up against the wall. His career was on the line. Caldwell wasn't here, and he had mistakenly discounted Maxwell. Now he could see that the lines of authority had shifted.

Dani saw the fear in Tom's eyes. She turned back to him. "What have you learned about yourself so far?"

Tom looked at her with new respect. "I see that I'm the one acting childishly. I don't like being told what to do, and it sometimes creates problems for me on the job — and at home. That's the truth."

"Do you see value in learning about yourself?"

Tom looked at her and nodded. "I do."

"Do want to continue learning?" Dani's voice was gentle.

"Yes," he replied without hesitation.

"Good. Stay open to what you see and feel." Dani's voice was smooth as butter. She turned and looked deep into Maxwell's eyes, like a cat laying its latest prey at her master's feet.

In that moment, Maxwell knew that his instincts had been on track. Dani was alert and observant. She had learned even more than he had expected. Still a little soft around the edges. He would have preferred a confrontation that resulted in Tom's removal, but toughness would come with time, and he would be the one to teach her. He stood up behind her and put his hands on her shoulders. "Dinner is ready."

~

Joseph Army had pulled several strings to arrange a private meeting with the vice president late in the afternoon, relying heavily on the fact that he had roomed with him during their sophomore year at Yale. It seemed so long ago, he thought. How young they were then, and naive. They thought they could do anything. Accomplish anything. He smiled. Back in those days the veep was one of the best party animals around, could chug beer with the best. But he was always ambitious, even then.

The vice president's secretary told him to go in, reminding him that he had only five minutes to complete his business. They greeted each other warmly. Army knew he had no time to waste so he jumped in. "Mr. Vice President."

"John," the vice president said.

Army was relieved that he didn't insist on formality. "John, my reason for coming here today is to ask you to call off the IG. You know Sinclair has been hounding us for the past three years. He's created such a problem with Congress that we can't get anything through appropriations. Now he's after our training program, which you know is top notch. We're finally creating the kind of leadership that we need and Sinclair is off on another of his witch hunts. This time his target is Caldwell."

"Caldwell." Exclaimed the VP. He had personally invited her to present workshops to his Council and had been impressed. "What's his problem with Caldwell?"

"Our take is that he's been listening to some disgruntled employees — a few who have flunked Caldwell's program. You know she likes to eliminate dinosaurs, but how the hell can we move the agency forward if we always lower our standards to the lowest common denominator? Since the strike, we've been trying to put this agency back together. We're finally on the right track, and now Sinclair's trying to single handedly destroy everything."

"Sinclair's not an easy man to sway, Joe." The vice president frowned slightly.

"I have something that might help." Army handed him a sealed envelope. "Go ahead. Open it."

The picture was that of a young, black woman in a most compromising situation. The vice president looked at him puzzled.

"Sinclair's daughter," he explained. "She's the pride of his life. These were from a rebellious period about twelve years ago. She's turned her life around rather well. Finished law school third in her class. They'd destroy her promising career as a prosecuting attorney, don't you think?"

The vice president looked like he had just bitten into a rotten fruit. Politics was distasteful.

"I'll do what I can, John." The vice president almost looked sad as he handed back the envelope and dismissed his old roommate.

~

The admiral was sampling the latest blends in an exclusive cigar shop in Arlington. He admired the maneuvering of the tobacco companies. While cigarettes had become politically incorrect, a brilliant marketing campaign had elevated cigars to the level of absolute chic. The campaign had begun in the media as celebrities publicly puffed cigars and were paid fortunes in cash and complimentary vacations in some of the finest resorts in the world for their informal endorsements. It was one more testament to the power of free enterprise.

A lilting bell notified the proprietor that another

customer had entered and he went over quickly to greet him.

"I'm here to pick up my order, Sam," Skippy said coming into the shop with a smile. It was a rare treat to be able to stop by personally. He looked back out the window, reassured by the limousine that waited for him. He had to be careful at all times. The proprietor dismissed himself, going into the back room of the shop to locate the order.

Skippy wandered toward the admiral. "Have you heard about Caldwell?"

"Yes. But Maxwell concerns me more. He's taken over her program — in the face of an investigation. It will bring unwanted attention."

"I fear Maxwell may be out of control. That's the risk we took in selecting a sociopath for our work. What a shame — so brilliant, yet so completely devoid of true discipline. We'd better take precautions until we know what he's up to and what his limits are."

"What kind of precautions?"

"I think the Trilogy should disappear, along with all her cargo."

The admiral nodded, his assignment understood.

Skippy looked at his friend with compassion. He knew that it hurt him to realize that Maxwell had let them down. "Don't take it so seriously. There are so many now, in every branch of government. There is no stopping the Second Ring now."

The admiral nodded. "I recommend this blend." He pointed to the counter where they were standing as the proprietor returned.

Chapter Twenty: Trilogy

The sturdy fishing boat lurched unevenly in the choppy waters of the bay. Bill's face, lit by the full moon, betrayed signs that his stomach was threatening to give up the contents of his latest meal.

"You don't look so good." Jake grinned. He had been blessed with a cast iron stomach.

"I'll be all right," Bill mumbled unconvincingly as he peered through the powerful binoculars. Through the evening mist he could see the Trilogy bobbing up and down. He wished the seas would calm down until they accomplished their mission. Their plan was to wait for the watchman to make his nightly visit into town. They would then bring the boat closer and swim the rest of the way. He and Jake were each equipped with SCUBA gear in case they needed to quickly disappear from sight.

Bill looked around the bay once more. It was a different place at night. The choppy waters were going to make their task more difficult, and they were making him urgently sick right now. He lurched forward against the boat's railing and heaved. Feeling much relieved at least temporarily, he returned to his lookout duties.

"Something's up," he cautioned at last. "Two men I've never seen before are climbing down from the yacht and getting into the launch, but there's no sign of the watchman. I don't like it." He kept watching, checking for any other signs of activity on the ship. "Jake, maybe we'd better scrub our plans for tonight."

"This might be our only chance. I say we go."

"You're right. Let's do it."

Jake piloted the boat slowly and not too directly toward the yacht, the slow chugs of the motor hypnotically marking time. He anchored a safe distance away with the bow facing the Trilogy to create a narrow silhouette and let them roll backwards into the water over the stern, hopefully out of view. Their wet suits had been difficult to put on with the motion of the boat, but they would be protected from the chilling waters of the bay, and the dark color would help hide them in the unexpectedly bright moonlight. They strapped on tool kits and, each man grasping his mask, rolled backward into the churning water. The cold water cleared Bill's head and his stomach seemed relieved to be away from the tossing boat. He struggled to keep up with Jake. By the time they had closed the distance to the yacht he was beginning to think he'd live after all.

"Let's find the watchman." Jake spoke in a hushed voice, as they hung onto the ladder. He looked up at the yacht's name painted in heavily scrolled letters. Trilogy. Jake made himself focus on the task at hand. They moved silently up the ladder and he whispered in Bill's ear.

"We'll do a quick once over." They split up and searched the ship systematically. It was a large yacht and took them several minutes to cover the state rooms, galley, and crew quarters. Bill was turning the corner of a long, narrow hall when he noticed a door slightly ajar. He silently inched down the hall, approached the door and peered in. As he scanned what appeared to be the main lounge everything seemed normal. He cautiously entered the room and walked the perimeter. Then he spotted an unmistakable form behind the large sofa.

Bill looked nervously around the room. Suddenly he glimpsed a dark form in the doorway and for a moment didn't recognize Jake. "Over here!" He finally whispered hoarsely. On the floor, sprawled on his side was the missing watchman. His white shirt was stained with fresh blood, and there appeared to be a single gun shot wound in the center of his forehead. Jake came to the door and followed Bill's startled gaze to the body. He knelt down beside the man and checked for a pulse.

"Dead." He said, confirming the obvious.

A quick but thorough examination of the room uncovered two hidden cameras with small lenses. An untrained eye could never pick them out, but Bill was familiar with surveillance and spotted them.

"Somebody put some money into this setup." Bill's voice conveyed admiration. "This is the type of surveillance equipment you'd expect to find in the bedroom, not the main lounge."

"I wonder where the recording equipment is located."

They checked out the staterooms and galley and found nothing. They finally found themselves outside the only locked room on the ship, a small room behind the main lounge. Bill took out a special lock pick. After several attempts, he finally jimmied the door. Once inside, his instinct led him to run his fingers along the cabinet moldings and under the bookcase shelves. Soon he discovered the fingerprint scanner.

"Look at this." Bill squatted down so he could get a look at the device. "I've heard about them, but this is the first one I've seen."

Jake didn't look. He was standing and frowning silently.

"What is it?" Bill asked.

"I don't know. Something's wrong. I feel it." They look at each other uneasily.

"Do you hear that?" Jake finally determined that the sound was coming from behind the bookcase. He heard it again, a regular, muted beeping sound.

"Let's get out of here," Jake commanded. "Now!"

They scrambled to the top deck, grabbed their SCUBA gear and jumped over the side.

As they leaped off the ship Bill's SCUBA gear was jerked from his grip, snagged to something on the railing they had vaulted. They heard the thud of a small explosion just before they hit the water. As soon as Jake came up for air, he slipped his mouthpiece into his mouth. Bill surfaced a moment later and began cursing his apparatus dangling uselessly from the railing above. Jake grabbed his shoulder and thrust his mouthpiece into Bill's mouth. Bill got the message and took a deep breath.

Through portholes in the side of the ship they could see flames beginning to spread to the upper deck. Realizing that their fishing boat was on the other side of the ship, Jake pointed down towards the dark water and shouted to Bill.

"Let's go under the ship and get back to our boat under water. No way of knowing who may be watching these fireworks." They disappeared into the cold darkness, staying clear of the yacht's hull. As they tried to reorient so they could swim towards their boat a fierce explosion, much larger than the first, ripped the boat apart. They were both temporarily stunned by the concussive force. Within seconds the surface of the water lit up and they could see a glow above them, as though it were daylight. Fire had spread over the water's surface, which was apparently now covered with fuel.

Peering around the murky water Jake saw objects, propelled by the force of the explosion falling into the water all around them. As his senses cleared he was aware of a high pitched ringing in his ears. Unexpectedly, a large section of hull landed a few yards away. The impact startled him and he was caught up by an odd sense of time collapse. He felt frozen in the moment, like a deer caught in the headlights of a truck. Slowly events began to pick up speed, like a heart that has to be coaxed back into beating after an attack. In that state, Jake found himself staring semiconsciously at an object floating downward, bobbing and weaving in slow motion as it descended from the surface to within a few feet of his face. He reached for it instinctively and slipped it into the neck of his wet suit. At that moment he remembered to hand Bill the mouthpiece. Bill grabbed it gratefully and took several more deep breaths. The whole experience took just a few seconds.

Jake knew they had to get beyond the range of the fire. They began swimming, pausing every few yards to take a turn breathing the rich air. Finally, they were clear of the fire and came to the surface, turning toward the sight of the burning wreckage.

"Five more minutes," Bill said, between gasps of breath. "That's all we needed. Just five minutes." He was dejected. They watched what was left of the Trilogy slowly sink as the last piece of burning wreckage flickered out. They were left in darkness.

They completed their swim back to the rented boat and climbed wearily on board. As they began to peel off their gear a small object fell to the floor of the boat. Jake picked it up and handed it to Bill.

"This looks like an audio digital tape. Where'd you get it?" Bill asked

"Strangest thing. It drifted right in front of me after the explosion, when we were under the flames. Is there any way to find out what's on it after what its been through?"

"Leave that to me. I know some technical wizards who can work miracles."

Now they at least had a next step.

~

Jake was standing in his underwear shaving in the bathroom of the hotel suite, wondering what angle to pursue next. The television in the background was updating him on the morning's news. He heard the name Virgil Sinclair over the sound of the running water and stuck his head out to see what was going on. The voice was familiar but somber.

"I regret to inform you that as of this morning, I have resigned as Inspector General of the Department of Transportation. My reasons for leaving office are purely personal, and have nothing to do with the recent investigation into the training of the FAA."

That was it. Short and sweet. To anyone familiar with Washington's chronic use of doublespeak, it was clear that Sinclair was out because of the recent Caldwell investigation. While Jake stood there, stunned, the phone rang.

"Did you hear?" It was Bill.

"Sinclair?"

"Yes. Somebody got to him. By the way, the tape turned out to be more than I had hoped. It's digital video. The techies are drying it off. They say it should be ready for us to watch in a few hours. Can you come down to the lab?"

"I'll be there."

Chapter Twenty-One: Surrender

Saturday afternoon held an unusual prospect for the participants of the training program. Everyone was scheduled for a half-hour private interview with Andrew Maxwell. The word, whispered in hallways, was that it had something to do with Caldwell's conspicuous absence. It had been made clear that on this rare occasion, everyone could get to bed early. Dani's name was last on the list. By the time the door opened and the last person to be interviewed emerged, flushed and determined to be the best candidate possible, it was late and Dani was deeply tired.

Maxwell sat behind the desk in the beautifully furnished study, elbows resting on the chair arms, fingertips arched against each other. He watched her enter, and gestured towards a chair facing him. There was a long silence as he studied her. Finally, he stood up, walked around the desk near her and leaned against it.

"You did very well this evening. I knew you would. I chose you the first time I saw you."

Dani looked up at him. "For what? You chose me for what?"

"You're one of the best actors I've ever met." His eyes seared into hers.

Dani looked confused.

"You can drop the routine," he said. "From the beginning, I saw through your goody two-shoes act. I've got to commend you though, it's a nice option. No one would suspect you were capable of anything devious. No one at all. It's all a matter of skill — acting skill." He paused. "But you know that."

"What do you mean, acting skill?"

"You even had me going, with that story about your parents drowning. Exquisite. You even touched me."

Dani looked at him. "Do you need me to be devious?"

"I'm just telling you what I see."

"You're the character disorder. Maybe you're not capable of seeing anything else in others."

Maxwell folded his arms, leaned his head back and laughed. Most people didn't dare to challenge him and he sorely missed the interplay. "No, not a character disorder, Dani. But certainly a character." He laughed again, then paused a moment, growing more thoughtful. "In this society, how do you distinguish sociopaths from senators — a character disorder from a congressman? How can anyone believe the mass media? How can anyone stomach the lies — or the bad acting?"

"I think we don't know what's real anymore," she replied. "We're so influenced by what the media tells us that we're not in touch with ourselves. We're cut off from what really matters to us."

"What matters to you, Dani?" His voice was soft as black velvet.

She looked at him and thought. "Freedom to follow my own conscience matters to me — freedom and justice matter to me."

He laughed at her. "Justice? In this world? You're a bigger liar than I thought, or a hopeless dreamer. Maybe in a thousand years if we keep evolving. Dani, don't you see? I'm not the one who's out of touch with reality here."

"I didn't say we live in a just world. I said that it matters to me. I agree that the system needs fixing, but I still think most people are basically good at heart and we can get there if we work together."

"That's a load of bullshit." His voice was harsh. "People are basically selfish. Always out for their own gain. Good and evil are irrelevant. No. It all comes down to control. In any given situation, the person in control is the one with the most options. It's as simple as that. That's why I wanted you in my program. You're quite skilled at controlling people's perceptions of you. You make them think that you're good, innocent. And underneath it all you're as ruthless as I am."

"You think you know me, but you don't." Dani looked at Maxwell.

Maxwell stood and turned the other way. He appeared to be thinking. "I know you better than you think" He turned and faced her. "I know that you went to Tucson and met with Jake Morrow. We traced your car rental forms one-way to Tucson. Yes." He nodded as he saw her eyes falter. "You overlooked that detail. I also know that Jake is alive and here somewhere in D.C. I know that he's the one who handed your file to Sinclair."

Dani's heart was beating wildly, wondering how he could have found out about Sinclair.

Maxwell noted slight beads of perspiration on her upper lip. "You think you know me, but you don't." His lip curled.

Dani's world was spinning wildly. "If you know all that, then why am I here?"

Maxwell came close to her. "I knew you were like me from the first moment I laid eyes on you. You and I are the same. There is nothing the two of us can't do together. No limits. We can save this world from itself. Give the masses the leaders they are crying for."

Dani didn't move. For a moment, a strange mixture of doubt and hope flushed through her. Could he be right? Could they transform the world? Make it a better place? In that moment the possibility transfixed her.

"There's no such thing as good or evil." He continued, his voice lower. "It all comes down to control. And in each moment the person with the most options, has the power." His eyes narrowed as he observed her. He slowly reached for the top buttons of her blouse and undid them one by one. He saw her stop the beginning of a gesture with her right hand and smiled.

Maxwell reached for the hand she had instinctively raised to strike him with, and kissed the inside of her wrist. Then, with a quick twist he pinned her arm behind her and kissed her on the mouth. Dani struggled, but felt sharp pain as he raised her arm behind her back. She willed her body to relax. He kissed her deeply as though making a brutal point, then laughed in triumph and released his grip. She gazed at him for a moment, wanting to strike him — to hurt him for his intrusion, but she realized that her anger was exactly what he wanted. It fed him and made him stronger. Without a word she bowed, as though leaving the dojo, turned and left the room.

~

A few days later Jake once again appeared in Sinclair's study. This time it was late morning. The windows were open and the sound of birds and a lawnmower off in the distance floated in through the open windows. Sinclair looked up from his desk to see Jake standing in front of him.

"You seem to make a habit of breaking into people's homes." Sinclair was irritated.

"They got to you, didn't they?"

Sinclair nodded. "They knew I didn't care what they did to me — so they let me know that they were in possession of a tape that could destroy my daughter. Bastards!"

"What are you going to do now?"

"Not sure. I haven't had time to think things through. I do know that this thing is bigger than Caldwell or Maxwell. This has connections all the way up to the vice president!"

"I have something to show you." Jake looked at Sinclair intently. He had a special hand held viewer with him to display the tape he and Bill had salvaged from the Trilogy. He handed it to Sinclair and showed him how to start it.

Sinclair held the viewer, leaning on the desk in front of him. He watched silently for several minutes, then put the viewer down. He stared at Jake.

"Where did you get this?"

"You don't want to know, sir."

"How do you rewind this thing?"

Jake showed him. Sinclair started the video one more time and watched and listened to the admiral initiating Andrew Maxwell into the Second Ring.

Sinclair looked at Jake "This raises more questions than it answers. What the hell is the Second Ring? Who else is in it? What's it's purpose?"

"This sure sheds light on Caldwell's power over the FAA," Jake replied. "It helps explain why everyone was so afraid to talk, or to challenge her. Some powerful players have been backing her all the way. Somebody who was able to stop you with a single phone call."

"Correction — somebodies. You know, I've heard rumors for years, but I never believed them." Sinclair was thoughtful. "Secret groups thrive on silence. On implications and innuendo."

"Yes." Jake looked directly at Sinclair. "That's why I want to take this to the public. Get it out in the open so people can have a look at it. I don't want to wait until they're so powerful, there's no containing them."

"It may already be too late. You do realize that you'll put yourself in extreme jeopardy by going public? They've already tried to eliminate you once. They won't want to fail a second time." Sinclair's warning also conveyed his admiration for the younger man. "What's our plan?"

After Jake left, Sinclair sat thinking for a long time. He loved his daughter more than life, but he could not stand by while forces hostile to everything he believed in were moving systematically and silently into place, ready to destroy her world. He thought a minute about what had changed. Why was he willing to risk it all now, yet had given up so easily yesterday? Then he realized that it was because he was no longer alone. Contact. It was contact with others who believed in the same ideals. How very important it was. And he thought about the man who had stood in front of him, the man who had taken this on before anyone else understood, alone and without support. What gave him strength, he wondered.

Meanwhile, in the white utility van parked around the block from Sinclair's home, a technician focused the remote listening and recording device. Every word had been captured. The relevant data would be transmitted to Andrew Maxwell. There would be a bonus in it for him. It wasn't everyday he uncovered a plot like this. He congratulated himself.

Later that evening, while Virgil Sinclair was at the Kennedy Center attending a concert, a rather ordinary looking car pulled into his drive. Four men got out and let themselves into the house with a recently made key. After hours of fruitless searching, they called it quits. One of the men stayed behind, pouring gasoline over the strewn objects on the first floor. As he left, he lit a match and closed the door. Within seconds, flames were reaching for the much loved collection of music that had taken Sinclair a lifetime to acquire. It devoured priceless pieces of African artwork, first edition books. The fire was brutally efficient.

By the time Sinclair arrived home hours later, the last fire truck was leaving, and a few investigators were wandering through the rubble of his home, gathering clues. Sinclair was frozen, his heart heavy and the strength he experienced earlier in the day drained from him. A whole lifetime had been taken from him in an instant. He stood there, broken, unable to understand what he was looking at. A single tear slid down his tired face. He just stood there.

Silently, a silver Corvette slowly pulled up to the curb. The door opened and a deep voice called to him.

"Virgil...Virgil Sinclair."

He turned, expecting to see a messenger of death. A large man was gesturing for him to get into the car. Sinclair simply stared at him, still not able to respond.

"Jake sent me," the man said. Finally, Sinclair faltered over to the car. He groaned as he lowered his aging body into the seat.

After a few blocks, the chief turned to him calmly. "We're being followed. Jake expected that." The chief picked up the pace and gained a few blocks on the pursuing vehicle. Then he made a sudden right, turned off his lights and pulled the car into an empty parking lot. Sinclair noticed another silver Corvette parked on the street squeal away. The tail rounded the corner in hot pursuit, spotted the moving Corvette and pulled by, never seeing them parked in the lot. The big man turned to Sinclair and cracked a broad smile. The

IG had met the chief.

Chapter Twenty-Two: When the Bee Stings

Dani was in the kitchen pouring herself a cup of coffee when the caterer's van pulled up to the delivery door of the mansion. She had learned to drink from Maxwell's pot and no one objected. The cook, whose name was Sky, was a pleasant middle-aged woman for whom the seventies had been a defining decade. Everything about her was natural. Her long brown hair was loosely braided. No makeup muted her rosy face. Her eyes gleamed with health and there was a kindness radiating from her that comforted Dani. She was about as impervious to the control games going on in other parts of the mansion as a mother is to negative feedback about a beloved child. Her purpose, as she saw it, was to provide healthy and nutritious meals for all. She was happy fulfilling that purpose and to anyone entering the kitchen, the smells of freshly baked bread bore witness to her contentment.

Sky went to the door and let the delivery man in. He easily carried in two large bags of vegetables as though they were filled with popcorn. He was facing Sky, making small talk. When he turned around Dani's eyes opened wide. There in the kitchen big as life, was the chief. His large figure was draped in the company's white uniform, his long black hair pulled back at the neck. He winked at Dani as he placed the bags on the counter where the cook was hastily cleaning a space for them. Dani continued to look at him, stunned. For so tall a man, he had slipped into the room quite invisibly. It was only as she recognized him that he got her full attention.

"Would you like a fresh cup of coffee?" She offered, coming to her senses.

"That would be real nice, ma'am." As Dani handed him a steaming cup and napkin, the chief slipped her a folded piece of paper, which she tucked into her jeans pocket.

"This is great." He commented appreciatively.

Sky smiled. "Thanks. You're new, aren't you?"

"Filling in for Roger. He's on vacation this week." He finished the coffee and put the empty cup on the counter. Then, tossing a genuine, "Thanks," over his shoulder, the chief disappeared out the back door.

Sky began unpacking the fresh vegetables and

spices. "Did you see the size of his hands?" She said to Dani, handing her a bag of groceries to put away in the pantry bins. "I've noticed that big men are often very gentle." She smiled when Dani nodded and began humming to herself.

At that moment Andrew Maxwell's voice preceded him into the kitchen. "What's going on?" He inquired casually. The lighthearted pitch of their voices had caught his attention. Dani looked quickly at the cook who smiled back at her.

"Girl talk, Mr. Maxwell." Sky replied with a twinkle.

Maxwell poured himself a cup of coffee and left the room. A few minutes later, Dani went into the pantry with the bag of groceries and read the note.

Tape of Sinclair's daughter in Maxwell's possession. Important. Tomorrow Press Conference!

Dani stared at the note. What did they want her to do? What could she do? Her heart started racing. Everything seemed to be coming to a head faster then she had anticipated. She shook her head and took a deep breath in an attempt to focus her thoughts. She needed to think clearly. There wasn't a moment to lose.

~

The group was scheduled to meet outside in the garden for a morning meditation. As they were settling in, Dani pinched the inside of her left arm firmly several times. The area turned red and produced a small swelling. She got up quietly and went over to Maxwell. "Bee sting," she whispered. "I'd like to put something on it."

Maxwell nodded with a slight frown. He didn't like any deviations from schedule, but a bee sting was understandable. He watched as Dani went into the mansion.

She went straight to the kitchen where Sky immediately started clucking sympathetically and recommended some baking soda mixed with water to form a paste. She quickly produced the necessary items and handed them to Dani.

"This will soothe the pain of that sting," she said reassuringly.

Dani thanked her. "I'll go to my room to put it on."

She knew the mansion was empty, so she went directly to Maxwell's study. Dani looked carefully down the hall, then entered the room. There was a bedroom directly off the study where he was staying.

She went in. Her breathing deepened in response to her increased adrenaline.

"Calm down. No one's around," she muttered under her breath. After scanning the room quickly, she went directly to the closet. At the bottom, next to his shoes, was a briefcase she had seen him carrying protectively. It had combination locks on either side. She tried to open it, but the locks held.

She thought for a moment. Maybe he had been in a hurry, or careless when he closed it. He was left handed, she recalled, which meant the right side would have the best chance of being unmoved. He would have turned the left side to secure it. There were three sets of numbers. She didn't change the left most number. The second number she turned up one space. The third number, two. She tried the lock. It didn't open. She thought she heard something in the hall. Beads of sweat began to form on her forehead. She waited. Hearing nothing, she move the third number one more click. The briefcase opened loudly.

"Good girl," she congratulated herself quietly.

Looking through the contents of the briefcase, she came to a large manila envelope. It was flat except for what appeared to be the outline of a small box. She opened it. Inside, the glossy picture of a young black woman made it obvious why the tape was so controversial. She took the tape and picture and slipped them into the waste band of her jeans. Then she went back to the study and opened the top center drawer. Seeing a small box of paper clips about the same size as the tape gave her an idea. She took the box, closed the drawer silently and went back to the bedroom. She heard voices downstairs that sounded like Maxwell and the cook.

"He's coming," she warned herself in a whisper. "Easy now." She stuffed the box of paper clips into the manila envelop and put it back in the briefcase. As she started to walk away, she realized she had forgotten to lock it. Her heart was pounding. She heard footsteps in the hall. She forced herself to go back and turn the left numbers exactly as she had found them and set the briefcase down.

She tried to make herself breathe. The pounding of her pulse and the sound of her breath seemed to block out everything else. She slipped into the bathroom between Maxwell's bedroom and study, forgetting to lock the door behind her.

Maxwell trusted no one, and Dani's brief absence aroused his suspicions. He left the group, confident that they would continue their meditation until he returned. He checked with the cook, who told him she had given Dani baking soda and that she had gone to her room to apply it. Maxwell knew which room she was staying in and went there first to check on her, but Dani wasn't in her room. She also wasn't in the common bath that several of the women shared. He headed for his study and saw the door to the bathroom shut. Maxwell quietly moved toward the door. Turning the handle quietly, he pushed the door open.

Dani looked up. "Oh. You startled me. I've had the darnedest time getting the stinger out, but I finally did." She triumphantly held up a tweezers she had found in his shaving case on the sink. "I'm sorry I used your bathroom, but I didn't have a tweezers with me and went looking for one." He glanced at the whitish paste on her arm.

"You'd better go join the group for meditation." He frowned. After she left, he looked around the room, but everything was still in place. He went to the window and looked down at the group below still meditating. He saw Dani join the group as though nothing unusual had happened. Half expecting her to look up at him with shame in her eyes, he turned and noticed that his closet door was slightly ajar. Frowning, he went to the closet and took out his briefcase. It was locked just as he left it. He unlocked it and looked through the contents. Everything seemed normal. He cautioned himself not to give in to his paranoia. He put everything back.

Late that morning, Maxwell called Dani to his study. *He knows*, she thought, her heart pounding.

"We're going to Daytona Beach this afternoon." His voice was brusque. "Get some things packed. We'll be there for a few days."

Dani looked at him. "Why Daytona Beach. What's going on there?"

"It seems that your friend Jake has just boarded a plane for Daytona Beach." He paused and looked at her slowly. His words sounded strange to her, and seemed to take on a new significance in the short distance from his mouth to her mind. Dani felt cold and disjointed, as though she was in someone else's body.

"It's quite a coincidence," He continued. "Virgil Sinclair is on the same plane. I wonder what they could be up to?" Maxwell smiled. He enjoyed the cat and mouse game they were playing. She would lead him right to Jake. He was sure of it.

Chapter Twenty-Three: Daytona Beach

Duke Winters came squinting into the store from the service area of his beachside Harley shop. The morning sun created a glare that even the tinted windows with their brightly painted advertisements couldn't keep out. He finally saw Jake, who was squatting down to read a magazine.

"It's for you." Duke grinned at Jake and pointed to the phone by the counter. He had been more than willing to provide Jake and his friends with a point of contact and moral support. As far as Duke was concerned, his obligation was simple. Jake had saved his son's life back in Tucson, and he owed him. Besides, he understood what it felt like to be outside the system looking in. While he respected the stand Jake was taking, his own cynicism convinced him that the man was fighting a lost cause.

Outside, the roar of bikes was building to a slow

crescendo as bikers from around the country began arriving, drawn to the city each spring like salmon propelled by a primeval homing instinct. Some came in pairs, some in large groups, many traveled alone. Some of the more experienced bikers hauled their expensive machines in the back of trucks that provided a place to crash in the unlucky event that they didn't find a room. There was a growing feeling of excitement.

Duke walked to the front door and scanned the swarming crowd. As far as he could see, bikini and leather clad bodies blended in a strange but colorful fiesta. It was rare to see so many tattoos in one place. The tattoos ranged from single words or small figures to entire bodies covered with sometimes exquisite, sometimes horrific artwork. The art of tattooing had come of age and was on full display, as biker babes stripped down to bare minimums and headed for the beach or cruised down the main drag. There was a strange blending of body piercing booths and hot dog stands. The sight of a young man with a gold stud in his tongue licking an ice cream cone sent a chill down Duke's spine and he shook his head and smiled.

Jake was relieved to hear Bill's voice on the phone. He had stayed behind in D.C., while Jake, Sinclair and the chief had come to Daytona Beach.

Their objective was threefold: First to lead Maxwell into an area he was not familiar with, and take the focus of the unknown men he was involved with away from D.C. That would free Bill to release the results of his investigation into the government cult. Fortunately, Bill still had friends at the Post.

Second, Sinclair had decided to keep his speaking engagement at a spring conference for aviators at Embry-Riddle. It had been arranged while he was still the Investigator General of the Department of Transportation. It would be his last public act, his swan song. He knew the speech would be covered by the local media, and had notified CNN and C-SPAN of the event. He knew they would be there.

Thirdly, and to Jake this had become the most important, they needed to get Dani away from Maxwell. It didn't take a rocket scientist to figure out that she was in grave danger, and that Maxwell was now using her as a pawn in whatever mind game he was playing. The thought of Dani being that near to Maxwell was of great concern to Jake. He had finally come to realize how much he loved her. They had to get her out before Maxwell realized the part she was playing.

"How does the IG like the new earpiece?" Bill's voice brought him back to the task at hand. They had fitted Virgil, Jake and the chief with special communicators that had both receiver and transmitter in the earpiece.

"We can't shut him up." Jake grinned. "It's a good thing we have volume control."

"By the way, we checked. The car that followed Sinclair and the chief the night of the fire does belong to one of Maxwell's followers. And Jake," Lee paused. "Dani left with Maxwell a few hours ago. They're headed for Daytona and should be at their hotel by now."

"I know. The chief is about to make contact. If she's got the Sinclair tape, everything's a go. And Bill — good luck with your story."

There was a silence on the other end of the phone. Then Bill said simply, "Take good care of her, Jake."

~

Andrew Maxwell was livid as he stood facing the two men who were sheepishly making excuses. They had followed Sinclair to Embry-Riddle where he was meeting with the president and getting ready for his speech later on in the day. More importantly, they had lost Jake.

"I think we can forget about Sinclair. He knows what we have on his daughter. We have nothing to worry about in that regard" Maxwell looked at them with disgust. "How many men do you have here in Daytona?"

"Five."

"That should be enough, if they're not all idiots like you." Maxwell was flustered. He really disliked having to depend on others. "I want to make this very clear. Find Jake Morrow. Is that understood? Come over here." He led them to the balcony, and they all stepped out, their mission immunizing them to the lure of the ocean breeze and white beach.

"That's the Band Shell. MTV is in town. It's biker week and Spring Break is starting. " Maxwell pointed to the left, just a few hundred yards away. They could see workers connecting wiring and putting final touches on the large outdoor screen, used for the MTV beach parties. They went back inside the room.

"There's no place for him to hide, and as far as we know, he's on his own and without resources. Use your technical people. Tell them to get their goddamn ears on and find him."

"What do you want us to do with him if we get him?"

"Not if. When you get him, fool. Just get him.

That's the most important thing. After that, get rid of him. I've had all I want of that Bozo."

They heard a knock at the door of the adjoining suite. Maxwell gestured for the men to be still. He went to the door. Dani was standing there dressed in a bikini and matching sarong. She was wearing sunglasses and carried a floppy bag with beach paraphernalia. Her long brown hair was pulled up playfully over her head.

"I'm headed for the beach. Care to join me?"

"No. Go ahead. Just be back in a few hours. Sinclair's talk is at 3:00. And remember, if you see Jake anywhere, let me know at once. Use this walkie-talkie. You can reach me any time at this frequency." He set it and handed it to her. Dani nodded and closed the door.

"Don't let her out of your sight for a second. Do you hear me?" Barked Maxwell. "She'll lead us right to Morrow."

Dani knew that he would have someone follow her, and as she left her room and walked down the hall she caught a glimpse of a short, nondescript man coming out of Maxwell's room. He seemed to be reading a newspaper. She decided to walk down the five flights of stairs to check her hunch out. Her suspicions were soon confirmed. As she completed one flight, she could hear his footsteps on the flight above her. When she reached the first floor, she passed through the lobby area to get to the wide back steps leading to the beach. The front desk clerk looked up and saw her.

"Ms. O'Malley. A message for you."

Dani went over and picked up the message. It was from the chief. He was here. She headed for the beach.

It was a glorious day. The sun was shining and for a moment it blinded her as she walked through the door into the fresh ocean air. She could see only silhouettes walking by, rays of sun filtering in between them. She moved slowly, shielding her eyes until they adjusted to the glare, then headed for the water as she walked out onto Daytona's famous hard packed white sand beach.

Dani stood in ankle deep water for a few minutes, smelling the salt air, enjoying the feeling of the sun on her skin and the soft sand underfoot. Picking up her things, she started to walk casually down the beach, heading north a few hundred yards. She then headed back towards the unending row of hotels, past the two lanes where the cars and motorcycles were allowed to drive on the beach and turned back towards the hotel.

She fell into the column of pedestrians, parading along next to the vehicles.

Cars, with young male bodies leaning out of every window, tooted their horns appreciatively as they passed. Dani found the concession stand mentioned in the chief's note. As she approached, the deep yet familiar voice of a vendor caught her attention.

"Ice cream sandwiches, only a dollar. How 'bout you, ma'am?"

Dani smiled and stopped. "That sounds perfect. I love ice cream sandwiches. Tax?"

"No, that's a dollar even."

Dani reached into her floppy bag and took out a dollar and the tape of Virgil's daughter.

"Thanks," the chief said. "Here's a napkin. That ice cream melts fast in this sun. Take two."

How could the chief, who was so obvious, be so invisible, Dani thought. He seems to take inordinate delight in it. His eyes twinkled in direct proportion to the outrageousness of the situation, and it made her smile.

She took the napkin and kept walking, biting into the sandwich with pleasure, relishing the cool vanilla taste of the ice cream. She read the message on the napkin, then wiping her mouth, crumbled it up and tossed it into a covered trash can. It said.

Lay low until diversion. Then walk south.

She reached her hotel and spread out the towel in her bag on the sand. She lay down and tried to let the sun calm her.

The man following her looked painfully out of place on the beach in his long pants, shiny shoes and short-sleeved shirt. He hadn't take his eyes off her, not for a moment. In fact, trailing Dani to the beach had been his best assignment in years. After she lay down, he relaxed a little. He eyed the almost bare healthy bodies romping on the beach and sighed unconsciously. Turning toward the hotel, he took out his cell phone and dialed Maxwell. "Nothing to report here, sir."

In the hotel room, Maxwell hung up the phone then dialed the local police.

"I want to speak to the officer in charge. This is a matter of utmost concern. An unbalanced man involved in several arsons in the nation's capital is about to assassinate Virgil Sinclair, the former Investigator General of the DOT.. I'd advise you to get several of your men down there to apprehend him. He's unstable and there's no knowing what he might do. Yes. This is Dr. Andrew Maxwell, director of training for the FAA. I'm staying at the Royal Suites. I'll meet you in the lobby of the hotel in fifteen minutes. I have a picture and a profile for your men."

~

Skippy left the small group of friends in his wife's capable hands and closed the door of his study behind him. He clicked a remote control and the radio of the small entertainment center settled on a country music channel. While the singer wailed in the background, he dialed slowly.

"Henry?"

"Just a moment," came the voice at the other end. He waited as the tenth richest man in the country came to the phone.

"Yes?"

"Henry."

"Skippy how are you?"

"Fine, thanks. Henry — Maxwell's lost it. He's completely out of control."

"Do you know where he is?"

"Yes. He's in Daytona Beach."

"I'll take care of things"

"Good. Just make it clean."

Within the hour, a lone figure stepped off a small

executive jet at Daytona Beach airport, where a plain brown car was waiting for him. The driver handed him a key for a room at the hotel and a small packet of information. There would be time to read the material and prepare. The cleanup was underway.

Chapter Twenty Four: Rebels and Loners

Dani rolled over and put her chin on her arms so she could get a better view of the crowded beach. She wondered what diversion the chief had planned. What contacts could he possibly have down here? Minutes went by. The sun was so relaxing that she started to drift off, when she heard angry voices coming from the concession stands. Two powerful biker women in the barest of bikinis were calling each other names and pushing each other, bumping into the surrounding crowd. One of the women, a well endowed blond, grabbed the overweight brunette by one arm and sent her flying into the sand. Humiliated, the brunette cursed, picked herself up and went after the smaller woman. The man tailing Dani appeared completely engrossed. Dani got up slowly, took jeans, a shirt and tennis shoes out of the beach bag and slipped them on quickly. She started walking south.

Three stories above, Andrew Maxwell scanned the beach and caught a glimpse of her moving quietly through the crowd. Using his cell phone, he called the man who was supposed to be following her, but there was no response. At that very moment, the well endowed biker babe careened into him sending his cell phone flying. He was completely engrossed in the colorful spectacle unfolding in front of him and never heard it ring as it lay in the sand.

Maxwell growled at the two men still with him in the room.

"Get all your men down there now. She's heading for him, I feel it. I want every one of you down there. I want them stopped! Do you hear me?"

They looked at each other, quickly checked their handguns and took off for the beach.

The walkie-talkie buzzed. Dani knew it was Maxwell, but waited a moment before answering. She turned and faced the third floor of the hotel. She could just make him out on the balcony. She pressed the button to let the signal through.

"Get back here — it's almost time." His voice was harsh. She knew he was trying to give his men time to catch up with her.

"Yes — it is time," she said, looking up at him. "Andrew?" She used his baptismal name for the first time. "You may have more options than me — but then I'm not alone." Dani look at him in the distance for a moment. She felt an unexpected wave of sadness as she looked up. A part of her knew she would never see him again. She understood that he was heartless and would eliminate her and Jake if given the opportunity, but for one brief moment all she saw was a little boy. He was so lost, she thought. Lost, a very long time ago. Her eyes moistened and she looked down at the sand on the beach. That's all any of us are, she thought.

"Dani!" His cry was unexpected. "Dani — don't leave me!"

She stiffened, took a deep breath and then exhaled. She dropped the walkie-talkie into a trash barrel without bothering to shut it off.

As she walked away, she could hear Maxwell continue to threaten her. "You'll never make it. You're don't know what you're up against. Do you hear me? You're out of your league."

She steeled herself and continued on. Up ahead

on her right, a lively game of beach volleyball was in progress. It looked like a group of bikers having a great time. As she got closer, one of the spectators on the sidelines left the crowd and approached her. It was Jake, at last. She ran toward him. It was almost over.

Jake gestured toward a large Harley parked next to a low beach wall. They converged, heading for the Harley. Jake seemed to be talking to himself, but as she heard what he was saying she realized he was somehow communicating with the chief.

"She made it," he was saying. "Sinclair? Good luck. It's in your hands now. We'll get in touch when we arrive at our destination."

At that moment three men in dark suits and street shoes cut them off from the bike. It was apparent that they were not there for fun in the sun. Jake stepped in front of Dani as one of the men pulled back his jacket to reveal a gun.

"Come with us quietly. We don't need any trouble," he said coldly.

"Not today," Jake said.

The man folded his arms and reached into his jacket, drawing his gun. With the gun concealed under his arm, he turned slightly and pointed it at Dani. "I think you will."

Jake looked at him intently. "No, I don't think so."

At that moment a volleyball came flying by the man's head, followed by a husky biker in hot pursuit. What looked like an accidental collision included a well placed elbow to the gunman's solar plexus, knocking him to the ground and driving this revolver into the sand.

"Now you did it," the burly biker who had spiked the ball said. "You made me lose my serve." He looked around at his buddies. "I don't like to lose my serve."

For a split second, the two men in suits looked dumbfounded at the man. Suddenly bikers swarmed all over them. Before they realized what was happening, a scuffle broke out and ended just as quickly. They had been stripped of their weapons and rendered harmless.

Jake placed his arm around Dani and guided her quickly toward the bike. Just as he was about to mount it, two more men in suits came up behind them. One spun him around. The larger man leveled a powerful punch to Jake's midsection. He went flying backward and landed in the sand. As Jake rolled into a crouch to regain his feet the man who had punched him took aim at his face with a drop kick. Jake deflected his foot. Rolling around, he brought his own foot into the side of the man's knee with such force that the man howled in pain.

As the man fell backwards, Jake saw the smaller man ushering Dani away with a gun against her ribs. But she suddenly spun into the man, deflecting the gun with one hand and bringing the other forcefully into his groin, followed by a round kick to his chin. She finished by picking up his gun, which he had dropped into the sand. Jake stood there in amazement. Dani looked at him and shrugged her shoulders with a mixture of pride and embarrassment and grinned.

Jake was still smiling at Dani when a dull noise rang out. His eyes suddenly clouded with confusion and he clutched his side. Dani saw with horror a red stain spreading between his fingers. She had not seen the man behind him fire his gun, but she saw him now, struggling to his feet, trying to take better aim at Jake. Without hesitation, Dani raised the gun in her hand and shot him in the leg. Several bikers were on him in an instant.

She ran over to Jake and pulled his shirt open. She looked up at him with relief. "It looks like it grazed you. Messy, but you'll live."

Jake nodded, but put an arm over Dani's shoulders. "We'd better keep on moving." They walked towards the big biker.

"Keep an eye on these guys until we clear out of here, OK?"

The biker laughed and took the gun from Dani. "Don't worry. We'll handle everything." Two bikers pushed the two men toward the wall next to the others. Then someone took a first-aid kit from their saddle-bags and patched Jake up with surprising efficiency. Someone else gave him a clean T-shirt.

"You two better get going." The big man laughed as he noticed the words on the borrowed T-shirt. Life's a Beach!

Jake looked at Dani. He had waited for this moment for a long time. He steadied the chopper and she climbed on.

"Where did you learn moves like that?" He said looking at her with admiration.

"I have many hidden talents," she purred. Leaning forward, she kissed him passionately. He swung into the saddle and she put her arms around him and held on.

~

The sound of a familiar voice coming from the television inside brought Andrew Maxwell back into the doorway of the balcony. There was increased activity by the Bandshell, and it couldn't be Jake or Dani. He knew that his men were handling them. Then he saw Virgil Sinclair on the TV screen.

"You wouldn't dare," he exclaimed under his breath. He went over to the table and opened his briefcase. He found the manila envelope and opened it. Reaching in he pulled out the box of paper clips that Dani had substituted for the tape. The photo was gone. He grabbed a pistol from the briefcase and ran back out to the balcony, his eyes wild.

"Good afternoon, ladies and gentlemen." Sinclair was addressing the reporters who were covering his speech at ERAU. "I want to stress that I am acting today as a concerned private citizen. As such, it is my pleasure to release to you the results of a private investigation into what has been called the Government Cult. I have a packet of documentation that we will hand out to each of you when I finish. Further, the Post, starting tonight, is running a series based on their in depth investigation into the leaders of that cult, a secret high level organization known only as the Second Ring.

"The effort of bringing the extensive influence of this cult to light has cost several good people their jobs, and others their lives. We owe them all a debt of gratitude. If they had not decided that freedom of thought, freedom of conscience mattered more to them than their security and comfort, we would not be here today." With that, Sinclair nodded, and the technician, a very large man with dark hair and strong features, began playing the tape of Maxwell's initiation.

Maxwell watched in horror, as his own voice drifted over the sounds of the beach.

"Belief is the only Truth. Truth brings Transformation."

The door to Maxwell's room opened slowly. A dark figure carefully closed the door behind him.

"Transformation brings The New Order. The New Order brings Justice."

The man advanced like a fast moving shadow. Maxwell was leaning over the rail, in denial. He did not understand what was happening. What could have gone wrong? He had everything under control. Without hesitation, the silent figure rushed forward, grabbed Maxwell by the crotch and shoulder with his leather gloved hands, and in a single powerful movement, hurled him over the ledge. There was a dull thud below. The man disappeared back into the room. He quickly searched the room, taking Maxwell's briefcase and leaving the luggage. He left a typed suicide note on the table explaining that Maxwell could not endure living with his guilt. Then he was gone.

"The Secret of the Ring is Belief. The Wearer is

Invisible."

~

At the family estate in Alexandria, the admiral was reading with his beloved miniature sheltie on his lap when the phone rang. He answered it and listened carefully. Without a word, he put the phone down and picked up the dog. He went down the hall to his bedroom and opened the night stand. There, in the drawer was a small vial containing three different pills he had been given by his devoted doctor in case the pain of his cancer grew too great to endure. He swallowed the pills and lay down on his bed with the sheltie for the last time. He had lived a good life. Maxwell had disappointed them. He never had understood the selflessness required of a good soldier. But there were others. The cause would go on. The admiral smiled. His heart was at peace knowing that the Third Ring was secure and that his was an honorable death.

~

Jake brought the bike to full throttle and then rode up the beach ramp and over to Duke's Harley Shop.

There were bikers everywhere. Duke, who was out front talking with a few customers, saw them and came over.

"We want to thank you for your help," Dani said.

"Glad to help. Where ya off to?

"I think we're going to disappear into the Keys for a while. We've got some catching up to do." Jake smiled and looked back at Dani.

"What about the others?"

"Sinclair and the chief should be walking away from the press conference..." Jake checked his watch. "Right about now. They're quite a team. Who knows what they'll take on next."

"Bill's investigative series is rolling off the press even as we speak," Dani chimed in. "I'd say he's on his way to one of those barefoot Caribbean cruises."

"I just hope he remembers to bring Dramamine." Jake laughed.

"Tell me." Duke took a step closer and looked at them. "Do you think it's finally over?"

"Over?" Jake shook his head. "I think it's just beginning."

"By the way, the local cops have an APB out for you guys. Apparently, you're armed and dangerous. Get this — they're looking for a guy and girl on a Harley. We think you could use a little cover." He winked and nodded for them to look behind them.

There, as far as the eye could see, was a line of biker couples. When Duke waved his arm, the column of bikes took off, passing them one by one, roaring by in all their raw glory. They revved their bikes and waved as they passed. Jake pulled out and they made way for them. They were immediately lost in the crowd.

The sound of rolling thunder quickened Jake's pulse. The machine beneath him vibrated with power. The sky was blue and Dani's arms were around him. He felt hope once again. Dani leaned back, holding onto him with one arm, undid her long hair and shook it free.

Chapter Twenty Five: Epilogue

Six months had passed since the Post ran his series on safety and cult issues in the FAA. A lot had happened Bill Lee mused, tapping his empty coffee cup with a pencil. Thanks to media attention a congressional committee had been formed to study the matter, and a preliminary hearing was held. But public interest waned quickly, and committee members turned to issues more likely to further their own ambitions. The FAA issues slid to the bottom of the house agenda like stones in a muddy pond.

After a discrete amount of time he was let go from the paper that had been his base of operations for eight years. A necessary cutback, his boss claimed. But Bill knew better. He had brought unwanted attention to some powerful men. This was the consequence and he'd have to live with it. He wondered who they were. The nameless men. The controllers.

Bill looked around the dingy little office. He had

picked up a P.I. license and did small jobs here and there, mostly surveillance cases for insurance companies. He went over to the window, drawn by the unusual amount of activity in the streets of the nation's capital. He glanced at his calendar. It was Saturday, October 4th. The Promise Keepers were in town for a huge prayer meet.

Behind him, the door opened carefully. He turned in time to see the janitor come in. But it was not the usual man. Much taller, with black hair pulled back at the neck. Bill's eyes lit up with recognition, but the chief gestured for silence and Bill followed him into the hall.

"The I.G. wants to meet you at the Jefferson Memorial in one hour." The chief smiled. "It's good to see you, friend."

An hour later, Bill found the I.G. standing on the stairs of the memorial. He walked over and stood quietly by him They watched as nearly a million men gathered devoutly on the mall. From the sound system, an occasional phrase or hymn drifted into Bill's awareness. He caught something about begging for forgiveness. The mass of men rose, then dropped to their knees as though they had one mind.

Sinclair got right to the point. "Have you heard of the Fund?"

"The FAA Fund? Yes. The airlines collect money through a ticket tax. The purpose of the fund is to pay the FAA for things such as airport usage, radar, weather reports, security and safety issues."

"Yes, that's right." Sinclair was pleased. Lee would be an asset to the team. "The monies are held in the Fund and invested. Much like an endowment. Well, until now Congress has controlled the Fund. They authorize the disbursement of monies each year, which frustrates the FAA. They blame their crumbling infrastructure on the micro-management of Congress."

Bill looked quietly at Sinclair. "They do have a point, Virgil. They don't get money when they need it. It takes so long to get a system funded that it's outdated by the time Congress agrees to appropriate the funds. And decisions are politicized. They're made on the basis of how to get elected not how to keep the public safe."

Sinclair nodded at this assessment. "True. The FAA has been working towards semi-privatization for several years now. The problem is, if the FAA is privatized, they will retain their own revenues. They will control the Fund -- without checks and balances. And we're talking billions of dollars here."

"Who will be in control of the Fund if the FAA is privatized?" Bill asked.

Sinclair smiled. "That is the question, son."

They walked down the stairs to the mall and were lost in the crowd of Promise Keepers. A strong voice from the outdoor stage rose in rhythmic cadence, grew louder and filled with emotion. It slowed to a measured pace and thundered rhetorically. "And everybody said Amen".

And a million voices s responded.

"Amen".